PERM

The Perversion Trilogy, Book Three

T.M. FRAZIER

FRAZIER

USA TODAY BESTSELLING AUTHOR

PERMISSION
The Perversion Trilogy, Book THREE

Copyright @ 2018 by T.M. Frazier
ISBN: 9780578423951

Edits: Karla Nellenbach, Last Word Editing

Ellie McLove, My Brother's Editor

Cover design & formatting: T.M. Frazier

Cover photography: Wander Aguilar

gritty world that rivals her King series! The characters, even the crew of secondary characters, are captivating, and the chemistry between Tricks and Grim is tangible and SCORCHING."

"OMG!!! What a story. It was dark, gritty, violent, and perfect. AMAZING!!!!

Always for Le3C
Forever & Ever
(of Evers and Evers Real Estate)

For BB Easton
#NOTMWAGTD

PERMISSION

per·mis·sion /pərˈmiSHən/

1 authorization

2 consent

"Nobody can hurt me without my permission."

— MAHATMA GANDHI

ONE

THERE'S A CERTAIN BEAUTY IN DEATH, IN WITNESSING life leave a body. One cycle ends while another begins. Much like a decaying flower shedding its last petal, or a dead, rotting animal, feeding the trees that take root in its bones. I don't claim to know where anything goes after it dies, or if once a final breath is exhaled, it's just like it was never there at the start.

Being on the giving end of death has always been easy for me. Thrilling even. I've never once watched someone die (who isn't part of my family or Bedlam) and thought, *No, they should live.*

The bleeding girl I'm carrying is different. This feeling inside of me is different. I want for her to live. Demand it. Will it even. I want to see her open her eyes, hear her take a motherfucking breath. To speak a fucking word, goddamnit! Not because I care about her, but because she's essential to Tricks's happiness, which makes the girl important to me.

It's a strange fucking feeling. Caring by association. I don't even fucking know the girl. Never spoke a word to her. Yet, I hope and wish with everything I am that Gabby will live.

There are so many things beyond a living, breathing best friend that I want to give Emma Jean Parish. I want to give her a life. A real life. A place of our own with a big kitchen, a huge workshop in the garage, and a writing room for Tricks.

Ever since she first told me about the stories she made up to escape whatever terrible fucking things were going on in her life, I pictured her hovered over a laptop late at night, typing furiously away on the keyboard and blowing locks of honey blonde curls from her face. She could write children's fairy tales or even a story based on her life. Tricks's imagination is something not of this world. It should be shared instead of being limited to just conning people. Although, Tricks's cons require both her brilliant imagination and a ridiculous amount of natural and learned talent. Her books could entertain people. Help them even. Whatever she wants to do, all I know is that she was made for something more in this world. I want her to thrive and succeed and be more than...*me*.

Another thought comes to mind. I want to run

toward the image as much as I want to shake it away. Tricks, growing big and round, carrying what would surely be our hellion of a child. But could we raise our baby in Lacking? A place where kids only play outside when they're at school, hidden behind tall cement fences, far enough away from the worry of being hit with a stray bullet.

I could take Tricks away, leave Lacking. And I would do just that, even though it would mean leaving my brothers. All things considered, it seems like the best idea of them all, but giving up Bedlam and leaving Lacking city limits, doesn't automatically mean all vendettas against me vanish with us. I could still be sought out for one reason or another, and again, Tricks's life would be in jeopardy, along with the imaginary kid. The one I'm currently having delusions about as blood spills down my leg, staining my bright white sneaker with red streaks.

I want to give Tricks that kid and that life. I want to make it possible for all of her dreams to come true. So far, all I've given her is heartache and fear, along with an inability to protect her from the people destined to make her life a living fucking hell when I've never known someone who deserves heaven more than she does.

Even if Marco wasn't around to threaten our every move, what kind of life could I really give her? I'm Bedlam, always will be. Sure, I've got money, a lot of it, stashed away in various places, but money doesn't buy safety or freedom, or peace of mind.

The thought of not having Tricks by my side for the rest of my fucking life hacks into me like a hatchet to my throat, hurting worse than the fucking bullet lodged in my leg.

Every time I take a step, it's as if someone is chipping away at my thigh with a fucking chisel.

I can't let my pain, physical or mental, stop me from getting to the reservation hospital. I've let Tricks down too much as it is.

I can't let Gabby die.

I won't.

Without a free hand, I kick open the double doors of the reservation hospital. They bang loudly as they crash against the walls. I carry Gabby into the small waiting room where Sandy and Haze look up from their pacing.

I hand Gabby's limp little body off to the waiting doctor and his team. They lay her on a stretcher and shout orders at one another as they race her back behind a door with the words RESTRICTED painted above the frame.

I yank off my hood and am greeted with Sandy and Haze's disapproval.

"That was some stupid fucking shit you pulled," Haze says, crossing his arms over his chest. "Going over to challenge Marco without even fucking cluing us in on your plan."

"It was the only way," I reply, exhausted from walking miles on backroads and thick brush.

"You could have clued us in. We could have helped," Sandy argues. I realize they're more upset than angry. The knowledge stings worse than my leg. I never want to hurt my brothers. I'd die first.

"Or, you could've both gotten killed, and you needed to be here for Marci." I look around. "How is she?"

Sandy's expression softens at the mention of Marci's name. "She's still unconscious but stable. Took a bad blow to the head. Doctors are keeping her under until the swelling in her brain goes down, but they ran some tests, and they think she'll pull through."

"Thank fucking Christ," I say, blowing out a long-held breath.

"Where the fuck is EJ?" Haze asks, looking behind me as if she's about to stroll through the door.

I shake my head. "Lemming. He stopped the fight and took her into custody, then the shooting started. Unfortunately, Gabby got caught up in the middle of it all and took a bullet to the chest. Also, Marco is still alive. Unfortunately."

"Looks like you're in pretty rough shape yourself," Haze comments. His gaze trails from the gash above my eye to the hole in my jeans and then down to the puddle of blood I'm standing in.

"Took a bullet to the thigh," I say, brushing it off. I have bigger things to worry about. I gotta get to Lemming and see why the fuck he's taken Tricks.

Sandy looks around, and I know he's looking for medical staff to tend to my leg.

"There's no time for that," I rasp.

"You can't help no one if you bleed out. Sit." Sandy pushes me down into a plastic chair.

A nurse looks at my blood-soaked leg. "I'll get a room ready," she says, shoes squeaking on the laminate as she rushes into the restricted area.

"How do you think you're going to get her out?" Haze scratches his beard. "If you take one step inside that station, you're getting locked up, possibly for life. In case you've forgotten, you're a fugitive, and we're out on bail."

I grimace as pain shoots from my thigh up my spine. "You think that fucking matters?" I grate. "I've got to get her out."

"What about Mona?" Sandy asks. "You see her?"

I shake my head. "Bitch was nowhere to be found. Not that I could see. There was something else going on that soaked up all of my attention."

"Like what?" Haze asks, taking the chair next to me.

"Like the wedding I walked in on."

"No…" Sandy's eyes go wide.

I nod. "Yeah, that motherfucker Marco was marrying my girl in front of all of Los Muertos." I fill my brothers in on everything that went on over at the compound. The second I've finished, the bell above the door rings, and our heads snap to the brunette standing in the lobby shaking. Her cheeks stained with tears.

I stand and ball my fists. The nerve of this bitch.

Mona.

"IS…IS Gabby going to be okay?" Mona asks on a whimper.

"Let's save some time here," I begin as Haze pats her down and pushes her into a chair. He tosses me her phone, and I check it for tracking. It's disabled. Even so, I throw the sim card to the ground, and Sandy smashes it with the heel of his boot.

"You can cut the fake crying shit," I tell her. "Save your bullshit tears for someone who doesn't want to kill you. What's your endgame, Mona? Why the fuck are you here?"

She shakes her head and swallows hard. "I've done horrible, unforgivable things. I know I have. I can't tell you how very sorry I am. Even though you won't believe me, I really am sorry. There's no excuse for what I've done."

I roll my eyes at her theatrics. "No, there isn't. Tell me why I shouldn't end you right fucking here and now."

"You...you'd kill a woman?" she stutters.

I'd laugh at her concern if I could bother mustering a smile in the presence of this manipulative, evil psychopath who makes me, of all people, look as sane as sunshine. I shake my head slowly from side to side and correct her. "I don't kill *innocent* women."

Mona sucks in a shaky breath, rambling as she exhales. "I just wanted to be loved. Accepted. When Marco took Gabby and EJ from the foster home, I was sent away like I was nothing. Nobody cared. After a few years, I thought I was completely forgotten. When I reached out to Gabby, she told me not to visit. I didn't think I had a family anymore until Marco called me at school one day. He told me that Gabby was in trouble and that it was all EJ's fault."

She sniffles, looking to her shoes.

"Marco said he needed me. That I was the only one who could save Gabby from all of the hurt EJ was causing by being a traitor. He had a plan to get rid of her in a way that would benefit Los Muertos. I thought I was doing right by Gabby. By my family." She grips her thighs with her hands and looks up to meet my angry stare. "I know it's wrong. Gabby didn't even know I was at Los Muertos for over a year. I told myself I didn't tell her because I had to carry out the plan first, without the distraction of my sister, but it's really because I couldn't face her." She closes her eyes tightly. "I promise, you can do whatever you want to do to me--I won't fight you but only after I know if Gabriella is okay."

"Hold the fucking phone," Sandy chimes in. "How the fuck was Marco marrying Emma Jean going to benefit Los Muertos in the long run?"

My gaze lands on a picture of Chief David above the reception desk. I think of the story of Camila and his unborn child. Both my rage and the reason behind all of this becomes far too clear. "Because of the tribal benefits," I answer for her. "Because Marco believes that Emma Jean is somehow Chief David's daughter."

Mona nods.

"No fucking shit," Sandy says, followed by a long whistle. "Thought his woman was killed while she was pregnant?"

"That's what I thought," I say. "Maybe, she had the kid , and maybe, it's EJ. Or maybe, this is a lot more bullshit."

"Being fed to us by a sociopath," Haze adds. "I'm going to go with lies, but this can easily be fixed with one simple little test."

Mona nods. "That's why he set you up with the Irish. He figured he could have them take out Bedlam and gain access to both the reservation and your gun business all at once." She fidgets with her fingers, pushing her cuticles back with her thumbnail. "It's not just that. He thinks himself in love with her. He's infatuated. She's all he thinks about. Talks about. *Yells* about." She rubs her temples. That's when I notice the fresh scars on her wrists. When she sees me staring she yanks her sleeves down and folds her hands between her legs.

"He's so in love with her that he left her out on the streets to die, raped her, and turned her own childhood friends against her?" Sandy asks, echoing my own thoughts.

Mona's eyes are rimmed with red, underlined by deep shadows. "Isn't it always the ones we love who we hurt the most?" She holds up her hand and offers me Emma Jean's locket.

I snatch it from her and resist the urge to strangle her with it. "Where is Marco now?"

"I honestly don't know. After the chaos broke out, I heard him talking with Mal about how I failed him. How he brought me to Los Muertos for no reason at all. That was when I realized he only cares about his agenda and himself."

"Redemption doesn't happen in a day," I point out.

"It does when you're listening to your brother tell someone that you don't matter. That you never did. That you could be dead, and he wouldn't even notice."

"Boo fucking hoo," Sandy says with a roll of his eyes. "Tricks almost died because of you. Gabby might die because of you. My ma is unconscious because of you!"

Haze kneels down by her side. "I understand you're feeling really shitty right now." He tugs at her chin and forces her to look up at him. "But you gotta understand, after what you've done...we don't give a fuck." He releases her and stands.

The nurse comes back to the waiting room and motions for me to follow her.

I look directly into Mona's big lying eyes as I give my brothers my orders. "Take her to the war room. Tie her to a fucking chair, and don't let her out of your sight. If she so much as takes a step in any direction you haven't led her, kill her."

TWO

IN AN EXAM AREA BEHIND A FADED BLUE CURTAIN, THE nurse cuts open my jeans to examine the bullet wound in my thigh. "I'll get the surgeon. This bullet has to come out." She turns to leave the room, but I grab her by the arm, stopping her.

"You do it," I grit through my teeth.

She shakes her head. "You'll need to be under for the procedure."

"No, I'm not going under."

"I'm not licensed to perform surgery," she argues with her free hand on her hip.

"My mother was a nurse before the hospital shut down, and she started working at the casino," I tell her. "I know that nurses follow doctors' orders, but I also know that a lot of the time, nurses already know what's best. You telling me you aren't capable of removing this bullet?"

She doesn't hesitate. "No, I'm telling you I'm not licensed to."

"This is the reservation. No one is going to come after you. Look, if you don't do it, I'm going to leave here and do it myself. Save me the trouble of infection, and just get this fucker out and stitch it back up."

She shakes free of my leg and inspects the wound. She stands back up like she's about to argue again, but I cut her off before she starts. "Miss, my girl is in trouble. I've got to get to her...please."

Her look softens. She rolls her eyes, then plucks two latex gloves from a nearby box and snaps them on her hands. "I'm warning you. It's gonna hurt like hell."

I lie back while she gathers tools on a tray. "I'm counting on it." The truth is, it doesn't matter.

No amount of physical pain can compare to how I'm already hurting.

She digs the scalpel into my leg, and I use the pain to focus on my plan, but what comes to me are three words on repetition. I recite them over and over again as she digs around and slices into my flesh.

Rage.

Revenge.

Redemption.

"There you are," Chief David drawls, as he steps into

the curtained off area and closes it behind him. "What the fuck is going on that has Marci, you, and Marco's sister, all taking up valuable space in my hospital?"

"You know I prefer house calls, but Gabby and Marci needed more, and well, I was already here. I didn't think you wanted any more of my blood on your floors."

The chief stands at the food of the stretcher. "How thoughtful of you, Grim. Appreciate you lookin' out for the tribe."

The nurse stands up, examining her work, making sure the bandage is secure. She takes off her gloves and tosses them into a red biohazard bin. She acknowledges the chief with a hand to her heart before turning back to me. "You're all set. I'd offer you some pain killers, but..."

"I'm good," I say, waving her off. "Thank you." I take out my wallet and shove several hundred-dollar bills into her hand.

"No, you don't need to," she says, trying to hand it back.

"Take it," Chief David tells her. "And thank you."

She folds up the bills and shoves them into the pocket of her scrubs. "Keep it clean. Change the bandages every six hours. You might be a little light headed from the blood loss. Drink something sugary as soon as you can." With a clipped nod to me and another hand over her heart to the chief, she's gone.

I sit up, and grimace. The pain from my wound

stings, but it's manageable. The chief hands me my shoes. I fill him in on everything that's led me to being patched up in his hospital while I lace up.

"I guess now is a bad time to tell you that Alby's been spotted in town. Or maybe, it's not a bad thing. How did your meeting with him go? You sort your shit out with the Irish?"

I shake my head. "They never showed."

"A no-show with the Irish is as good as a bullet with your name on it," the chief says.

I give him a hard stare. "I know that. If they didn't show for the meeting and give me time to explain myself, it means they've already drawn their own conclusions." I reach for my jacket on the side table. I stand and shrug it on. "There's something else I have to tell you. Marco. I'm sure he thinks that Emma Jean is a member of the tribe. More specifically, your daughter."

"What the fuck?" The chief blurts, taking a step back as if I shoved him.

"Just think for a minute. Is there any way that Camilla had the baby? Even if it seems far-fetched, is there any possibility, at all?"

The chief thinks for a moment, closing his eyes. "She disappeared without a trace. I suppose it's possible she had the baby and survived for a time, but there's no way Fernando didn't eventually catch up to her. She would've found a way to get word to me if she were still alive. I'm as sure of it as I am sure I'm standing here talking to you."

"Emma Jean could be yours, then. If Camilla had the baby and hid her away somewhere before Fernando got to her."

"It's…I guess it's possible," the chief says. "Are you saying you think Marco wanted her tribal benefits?"

"And to have an in with the tribe so he can take over Bedlam's business here. It would explain why he's so adamant on his vendetta against us, besides his obsession with Tricks."

"Well, they'd have to be married," he laughs, although he stops when he sees the angry expression on my face and my jaw, which is clenched so tight I might break my own damn teeth. His laughter is replaced with worry. "She didn't marry—"

I cut him off. "Not willingly, but Marco gathered witnesses. The ceremony was done. I don't think her signature ever made it to the license, at least, not entirely, but I wouldn't put it past Marco to forge it so he can get his hands on her tribal benefits."

"Fuck. Desperate, isn't he? But she would contest it, surely, and say she didn't enter the marriage freely. The tribe may consider marriage unbreakable, but only one that is true. This plan of his, it wouldn't work." He lowers his voice to a grumble.

"It would if she wasn't alive to contest it." The words make me feel sick.

"No, there's another reason why that wouldn't work, but that's not important right now. Let's just say it would work. If Marco wanted to collect Emma Jean's benefits, he'd have to send in the marriage license with her blood test. If not, and he submitted separately, or at a later date, then he wouldn't be eligible to receive her benefits at the time of her death." The chief scratches his jaw. "I'll call the office and ask them to keep an eye on all recent submissions. If he's sent it in, or when he sends it in, you'll know your theory is correct, and more importantly, we'll have her blood on file to test against mine, but you might want to give me something of hers just in case, so we don't waste time and I can find out for sure if your girl is my blood."

"Like what?"

"Hair. A nail file. Shit, even her toothbrush will work. The lab on the reservation is state of the art. Top of the line everything. The tribe has spent a lot of money on the lab to ensure that a lot more doesn't end up in the greedy hands of outsiders. We gotta make sure those claims of heritage are real."

"Outsiders like me?" I ask, raising an eyebrow.

"Nah, I tested you a long time ago. Was kind of hoping you were of tribal blood. Half the time, I feel like you're the bastard son I never wanted."

I laugh. "Is that a compliment?"

He shrugs. "If you want it to be."

"Out of curiosity, how often do applicants ever test positive for being a tribe member?" I ask, adjusting my jeans. Thankfully, since the nurse sliced them open, the fabric doesn't rub against my wound. I shove my feet into my bloody sneakers.

"A lot less often than you'd think. Rollo was the last one and that was several months ago."

"Rollo?" I ask. "As in Rollo, one of my men?" I ask, wondering how I didn't know this.

"One in the same." He says. "He put in the test, but never the application for benefits. I asked him why once, he just shrugged and walked away."

The situation with Rollo is odd at best. I wonder why he never told me about being a member of the tribe. It's definitely something I remind myself to ask him at a later time, but right now I've got other shit that needs to be handled.

"Walk with me to the brothel. I'll get you something of hers to test," I say.

"Then, what?" the chief asks, walking beside me.

"Then, I've gotta get with Lemming and see what I can do about getting Emma Jean free."

"What charge is he holding her on?"

"Not sure, bullets started flying, so I couldn't make out his words. Whatever it is doesn't matter, I've got to get her out. If she goes to County, Marco can get to her in there. She won't be safe."

The chief's forehead wrinkles. "Not so fast there, son. You're juggling a lot of moving parts in those tattooed hands of yours. The task force will take you in the second you leave this reservation if Marco or Callum don't take you down first. I don't know if you've heard, but blood has been spilled all over Lacking in the past twenty-four hours. Margaret is ducking bullets seven ways 'till Sunday. The war has begun, and you, my friend, are at the center of it all. You need a plan, and a good one before you head out into the wild west our streets have become."

I pause and think, rubbing my temples. "What I need is a good reason why no one will be looking for me, at least not for a while."

The chief grins and claps me on the shoulder. His eyes brighten.

"What?" I ask.

"We have an old saying in the tribe." He leads me out the back door of the hospital and walks with me as I limp across the field toward the security buildings that house the Bedlam war room. He stops when we reach the building to face me, sparking an idea in my mind that leads to an all-out blaze.

"The living don't look for the dead."

THREE

DRIP. DROP. DRIP. DRIP. DROP.

The leaking bathroom faucet is the only sound in this otherwise silent room. I expected Lemming to bring me to the police station, but much to my surprise, I've been sequestered in the back bedroom of a house. The task force standing guard at both the door and outside the window.

I pace the room as I worry about Grim and Gabby. When the pacing doesn't help, I busy myself by exploring my surroundings.

It's a big room with its own bathroom. The master I suppose. It's clean and compared to what I'm used to, downright luxurious. There's a fully-stocked bookcase lining one of the long walls and a flat screen TV above the dresser. The bathroom has a large, soaking tub separate from the shower. Lining a shelf above the toilet are new travel-sized everything. Soaps, hair products. There's even a clear makeup bag filled to the brim with never-used eyeshadows, mascaras, and items I don't even know what they are for. There's a blow dryer hanging from the wall, and below it, rows and rows of lotions of all sort. Perched on the corner of the tub is a stack of folded fluffy white towels. The massive bed is covered in more throw pillows than I've ever seen. The comforter is covered with girls' clothes in various sizes with tags still attached. Sundresses, jeans, shorts, and even some vintage-looking band t-shirts. Next to the bed is a row of shoes. Three pairs of sneakers. Three pairs of sandals. Three pairs of flip-flops. Three pairs of boots. All the same, just different sizes.

It's been at least an hour. Still no Lemming. No explanation of why I'm here. I'm covered in dust and dirt, and my bones ache as exhaustion takes hold.

I sit and then stand, then sit again. Growing more and more frustrated as the minutes tick on. I stand and head into the bathroom. I might as well take advantage of the room while I wait for my captures to decide if they're going to fill me in on what's to become of me.

Luxury before torture? Pampering before prison? However you want to label it, I occupy my time by taking a long, steaming hot bath that soothes my aches. I shave. Wash my hair. After I dry off, I try a lotion that smells like cucumber, slathering it all over my legs and arms.

I wrap my head and body in the fluffy towels and go back into the bedroom. I choose a pair of yoga pants and one of the vintage band t-shirts. I dress and lay down on the bed. I'm picturing strong, tattooed arms and black roses as exhaustion takes hold and I drift off to sleep.

I'm not sure how long I've slept, but I wake to Agent Lemming pacing the room at the foot of the bed.

"It's about time you showed up," I say groggily, sitting up against the pillows and rubbing my eyes. I'm just about to ask him about Grim and Gabby, but I don't get the chance.

Agent Lemming stops pacing. His eyes are wide, and his expression is that of shock. "He's dead. They're all fucking dead," he whispers, like he can't believe it himself.

"Who?" I ask, dread climbing from my gut to my throat. I swallow it back down. I'm instantly awake. I jump to my feet. "Who is dead?"

His eyes meet mine. "All of them. Grim, Sandy, Haze. They're all fucking dead."

FOUR

"Why are we here?" I ask Agent Lemming.

"Protocol," he says, looking up to a camera perched above the door next to a sign that simply reads MORGUE. "Someone has to identify the bodies. Marci is at the reservation hospital. She's going to be okay, but she's still unconscious.

Marci. My own grief spreads to her.

She's lost everyone. Her husband. Her sons.

"I think I'm going to be sick." I grab my midsection where my gut feels like it's swallowed my heart and is now rotting inside.

"We'll make this quick," he assures me.

"I don't want to go in there," I say, taking a step back. I shake my head. "This can't be real."

He sighs. "We won't know if it's real until we go in."

Lemming pushes open the door and guides me inside with a hand on my back.

Three bodies wrapped in black plastic body bags lay side-by-side on stainless steel beds. The bags lay unzipped just enough to reveal the frozen faces inside. The morgue smells not of death, but of whatever chemicals they use to disguise death. A combination of vinegar and disinfectant that singes my nostrils.

Lemming looks to the ceiling again, scanning it briefly. He clears his throat and stands straight with his shoulders back. "Do you know these men?" He positions himself behind their heads and in front of a massive, body-sized filing cabinet.

It's a stupid question. He knows that I know them, but it must be part of his protocol.

I stare at the three men and take a step back. Not because I don't know them. Of course, I do. But it's as if I've been tossed into a fire, and I'm burning up from the inside out.

"It's okay. They can't hurt you. Not anymore," Lemming says, not realizing that he's got it all wrong. But correcting him is the last thing on my mind. He motions with his hand for me to come closer.

I steel myself and take one step and then another, propelled only by my need to get this hellish nightmare over with. Any second now, I'll wake up. I'm sure of it.

I approach the first table. My knees buckle. Agent

Lemming rounds the bodies and holds me upright with his hand under my elbow. "Do you know these men?"

"Yes. It's...it's them," I say, choking on my words.

"I'm sorry, but I'm going to need you to say their names out loud for the record," Agent Lemming says apologetically. He's a prick, but at this moment, I really do believe he feels sorry for me.

I look from frozen face to frozen face, willing them to wake up.

"Names," Lemming prompts.

I raise one shaky finger and point to the first body. "That's Sandy," I whisper. My eyes would well up with tears if I had any left to cry. I move my hand over to the body on the other end. "I know him as Haze." My heart pounds as I shake loose of Agent Lemming's hold and find myself standing over the body in the middle. He looks peaceful, as if he's sleeping. All the hard lines of anger and hurt typically marring his forehead and around his eyes are gone. His usually tanned skin is now a vampiric shade of harsh white. My stomach rolls.

"And this one?" the agent asks, coming to stand beside me.

My heart falls into my stomach, and again, he has to hold me upright. I can't stop myself from reaching out to the body, smoothing back his light brown hair that looks almost orange under the harsh fluorescents. The zap of our connection is still there, even in death. I hold one hand over my mouth, afraid that if I release one sob the floodgates will open to a lifetime of despair I won't be able to control.

"How?" I manage to ask.

"Not sure yet. The coroner hasn't finished his report." Lemming points to the last body, the one I've yet to identify. "And him?"

My bare thighs press up against the cool metal of the table. It vibrates against me, but it's not the table that's trembling. It's me. "That's...I mean he's..." I start. "This is Grim. Tristan Paine," I croak. I bend over and lower my lips to Grim's cold ear. I press my palm to his unmoving throat. My voice is a mere whisper he can no longer hear. "My honor. My loyalty. My love. My life. For you. For us." A tear falls from my chin and lands on his eyelid, spilling down his face as if he's the one who's crying. I wipe the tear with my thumb and press my lips to his. "For always."

Down the hall, someone is singing softly. The tune is all too familiar.

I stand and listen closely to make sure I'm hearing right. I am.

Too-ra-loo-ra-loo-ral
Too-ra-loo-ra-li
Too-ra-loo-ra-loo-ral
Hush now, don't you cry

Too-ra-loo-ra-loo-ral

Too-ra-loo-ra-li

Too-ra-loo-ra-loo-ral

The song grows louder. Closer.

An odd awareness crawls up the back of my legs like a hundred tiny spiders. My entire body is chilled, and not because I'm standing in a freezer meant for the dead.

Both Agent Lemming and I turn toward the sound. The top of a man's head appears through the high square window in the door.

Agent Lemming doesn't appear as alarmed as I do that there's a mysterious man on the other side of the door. Then again, he isn't hearing a life-long familiar tune outside of his own head for the very first time. The door swings open and in walks a man wearing a neatly pressed black suit with a white button-down shirt. No tie. He lifts the flat cap from his head and steps into the room. He's wrinkled around his eyes and his jaw is rough with stubble. His teeth are slightly crooked in the front, but it doesn't stop him from grinning wide at Agent Lemming.

All thoughts of the familiarity of the song fades. I don't know this man, but Agent Lemming apparently does.

"Cameras are disabled," the man informs Lemming.

"Good." Agent Lemming wraps the man in a one-armed hug. "Alby, good to see ya. 'Bout time you be

27

gettin' here. You get stuck in the jacks?" For some reason, Agent Lemming no longer sounds like a man from the South. He has a thick accent. One I haven't heard him use up until now.

"You got that fecking song in my head, again," Alby groans with a broad smile and the same thick accent.

"It's always in mine, Alby. You might get used to it."

It hits me. The accent, it's…Irish.

Shit. I check for the nearest exit, but they are standing in front of the only door. I could make a run for it. It might be my only chance of escape.

"Jaysis, this whole thing went arseways for Bedlam, didn't it?" Alby muses with a whistle, taking in the corpses of Grim, Sandy, and Haze.

"For them, yes. For us? We got what we came for." Lemming steps aside.

Alby's gaze lands on me. "Ye found her," he whispers, unblinking.

"Aye," Lemming nods proudly. "And not a moment too soon."

I momentarily forget my plan of escape and give in to my overwhelming curiosity. "You found who?" I ask, crossing my arms over my chest. "And by the way, nice accent, Lemming."

Lemming responds with a knowing smirk.

Alby laughs, gripping his midsection. "She's got fire, I see. It's practically smoldering from her ears."

"That she does," Lemming agrees, grinning like a Cheshire cat as he stares down at me.

"I'm in the room!" I yell, feeling my face redden. "Or can't you see me?"

Alby slaps him playfully on the back.

Lemming nods to me. "I see you perfectly. Clear as a lake on a sunny day." He turns to Alby. "Is the plane ready?"

Alby looks to the bodies again then nods. "'Course, Callum. Just as ye asked."

I gasp. My heart stutters, and so do my words. "Ca-Ca-Callum?"

"Yes, as in Callum Eagan." Lemming's eyes lock on mine. "The one and only."

FIVE

"How?" I manage to ask. We're in a well-appointed town car with soft leather seats. Lemming is seated next to me in the back. Alby is driving. "How did Grim not know you weren't really Lemming?"

"Simple. Never met the man. I've met Belly and Marci, but never Grim. He's always dealt with Alby when it came to our business."

"But you took Marci in. Had her arrested. Wouldn't she have recognized you?"

"I never went into the holding area. Never talked to her, just the boys who I also had never met as Callum Egan."

"Why? Why all this elaborate ruse?" I press.

His expression is one of amusement, his eyes as wide as his grin. "You'll find out soon enough."

We are silent for the rest of the thirty-minute trip. I feel like I'm in another world. Callum says he'll explain everything on the plane, but where that plane is going and why leaves me asking myself a million questions I can't answer while Callum is furiously tapping away on his phone while Alby drives. We pull up to an airstrip where there's only a single jet on the runway with the steps pulled down. Callum gets out and greets the pilot while Alby gets the bags from the trunk and begins carrying them over to the plane.

I pause as the grief clouding my thoughts clears. These men are Irish. Clan Egan. The same Irish men who think that Bedlam took down their shipment. They probably are the ones who killed Grim and his brothers. Lemming might have appeared shocked when he told me about their deaths, but then again, it was all an act. There was never really an Agent Lemming.

What if I'm next?

I can't die and leave Marci and Gabby with no one.

Unless, they've already gotten to them…

I push my growing panic down and form a plan.

Callum stops when he realizes I'm not following and turns back, waving me forward, I take a few steps toward the plane then stop. "Hang on one sec," I say. "I forgot my…" I let my words trail off as I slide into the back seat.

"What did you forget? You don't have anything," Callum shouts over the roar of the jet engines.

I don't bother shutting the back door. I crawl over the dash into the front seat. Thankfully, the keys are still in the ignition. I turn it on as Callum and Alby race toward the car. I throw it into reverse and slam my foot on the gas. I don't bother to look in the rearview as I speed through the bumpy field. The back door thankfully shuts from the bouncing around.

I don't underestimate Callum. If he has nefarious plans for me, then obviously, he's the kind of man who will catch up to me and will find me, but hopefully, it's not before I make sure Marci and Gabby are safe.

I turn out of the field onto the two-lane road. The tires skid in the dirt, and I correct the wheel until I'm straight once more. I only know how to drive because I was taught by one of Marco's soldiers who wanted me to drive the getaway car while he robbed a private poker game. It never came to fruition because he died, but I'm grateful I know the basics, even if it's been a while.

After what seems like forever, I spot the sign for the reservation on the side of the road. A peeling, short billboard with Chief David's smiling face standing in front of a backdrop of the casino. I pull on the wheel just as the driver's side window cracks into several small spiderwebs in quick succession.

Bullets.

I'm being shot at.

Thankfully, this car seems to have bulletproof windows because they haven't penetrated the glass. But bulletproof only lasts for so long when you're being hit over and over and over again. Eventually, the windows will give out. A tiny piece of glass falls onto my lap.

Soon.

I press my foot to the gas. I'm mid-turn, and as I straighten the car, the front windshield receives the same bullet decoration as the driver's window. I can't see anything. My adrenaline spikes.

Just stay on the road. The reservation is only a hundred yards away. You've got this. You can do it. Just keep going.

A tire pops, or at least, I think it does because the smooth road suddenly feels like I'm traveling over a minefield of boulders. The wheel fights my grip. I can't keep it straight. I lose control as the entire vehicle rattles and vibrates with the onslaught. Metal crunches all around me. The sound echoes in my ears as I careen off the road and crash into a steep ditch.

The airbags feel like a cannon being launched at my face, but I don't have time to access injuries as the bullets grow louder faster, continuing to pummel the car like the hail of a thousand windstorms. I crawl over to the passenger seat and try to unlock the door just as the driver's window explodes and rains down glass all around me. I duck and curl my body up as tightly in a ball as I possibly can under the dashboard as shots wiz only inches from my head. The passenger window breaks.

That's it. It's over.

I'm done.

Bullets aren't what broke the window, but a black, leather-clad elbow. It recedes as a tattooed hand appears, unlatching the door. It's twisted metal, but with inhuman strength, it's pried open.

Grim appears.

I must already be dead.

"I've got you, Tricks. Keep your head down." He reaches inside and pulls me out, tossing me over his shoulder. I spot Sandy and Haze to the right and left of the overturned car. They're returning fire. Grim uses his free hand and grabs his gun from his waistband, doing the same. Sandy and Haze cover for Grim as he moves us backwards until we're deep in the thick of the woods. He holsters his gun and flips me forward, cradling me in his strong arms.

He's running as bullets echo through the trees.

I reach up and touch his face, then nestle into his warm chest. "You're beautiful, you know, even though you're dead."

SIX

I WAKE UP IN A HOSPITAL ROOM, BUT NOT IN A hospital bed, on a small sofa. I glance up to see Marci occupying the bed in the center of the room. I made it. How did I get back? I think hard. Grim.

My heart sinks as I remember him cold in the morgue.

It couldn't have been Grim. He's dead.

It was all a cruel joke played on me, courtesy of desperation and hallucination.

I slink off the couch toward Marci and reach for her hand. I hold it in mine. "I'm so sorry, Marci. About all of this. About what happened to you, about losing…" I choke up, "…your boys."

"Our boys," she corrects me.

My eyes dart to hers. They're half-open. She squeezes my hand. Her smile is tight lipped.

"You're awake," I croak out.

"Am I?" she says with a small laugh that leads to a cough.

"You should rest," I tell her.

"I'll rest when I'm dead."

I flinch at her choice of words.

"And you've got nothing to be sorry about EJ. You might be the cause, but it's not your fault. You never asked for this. You never inserted yourself in our lives and asked us if you can be a part of our family. You just are." She laughs. "Belly had a saying." She squeezes my hand again. "Stop pointing fingers at yourself, and start pointing guns at others."

I raise my eyebrows. "That's...kind of confusing."

"Is it. It also never made a whole lot of sense...until now. Look at that. Belly was a goddamned philosopher after all."

"Marci, about the boys," I start, knowing she's about to take back her words about things not being my fault when she finds out her sons are all dead.

"Don't be apologizing about them either. They love you, and they'll do anything in the world for you, just like I would."

"I know they would've. It's just that— "

"If you don't believe me, you can ask them yourself. Sandy was just in here giving me shit about not wanting anything to eat yet. I'm sure he'll be back to annoy me again any second now, and tell him..." her voice trails off. Her eyes close, and within seconds, her breathing evens out as sleep pulls her into its embrace once again. Marci thinking she just saw Sandy is a fresh, gaping wound to my heart. It looks as if I'm not the only one hallucinating.

I slowly get off the bed and pull my hand from Marci's. I spy the bathroom. Once inside, I close the door. The click of the lock is like a hammer to a fish tank. Everything spills out from within me. I sink to the floor.

There's a wide crack running through the tile. It starts at the toilet between my feet and travels through the grout, splitting the floor all the way to the wall opposite me. I keep staring at it, hoping that, maybe, if I concentrate on the jagged line long enough it will crack open and swallow me down. I don't care where it goes.

Anywhere but here will do.

I pull my knees up to my chest and exhale a shaky breath. I feel so heavy. Everything feels heavy. I pull myself to my feet and lean over the counter, bracing myself on my elbows until my nose is almost touching the dirty mirror.

I glance at the reflection of someone I haven't seen in

a while. Me. My natural, curly hair, in all its rebellion, is starting to kink, resulting in the tangled, blonde mess now surrounding my face. I run my hands over my face, digging my fingernails into my skin. I want to claw it all off and not be me anymore.

What the fuck are you doing, Emma Jean? asks a deep masculine voice from inside my head. I stop my fingernails from drawing blood and set my hands back down on the counter. My sadness begins to morph into anger.

"Fuck off," I answer, shaking my head and closing my eyes. "You don't get a say in my life. Not anymore. You don't get to question me." Tears prick at the back of my eyes, but I sniffle hard and stand up straight, determined to silence his voice because it's not real. It's a lie. He's not here and never will be again.

You can't get rid of me, Emma Jean. I'm a part of you, the voice angrily reminds me.

"No!" I yell, sending my fist through the mirror. He's right, but I don't want him to be right. I want him to be ALIVE. "You WERE a part of me. You're not shit now. You left me. You're dead! You promised you'd never leave me, and now you're fucking dead! I fucking hate you for dying. For leaving me alone. Do you hear me? I fucking hate you!" I scream louder, kicking the cabinet until one of the doors gives way and falls to the ground.

My screams turn into a sob. I sink back down until

my ass cheeks hit the cold tile. I raise my knees to my chest and drop my head onto my forearms.

"I hate you so much," I whisper.

I could say the words a thousand times, but it's a lie no one would ever believe, including myself.

I take a few deep breaths and stand. I open the door, but just as I take a step back into the room, I'm pushed back inside by a wide, hard body who kicks it shut. I'm pressed up against the sink and a warm hard chest. I look up and freeze. I'm hallucinating. I have to be.

My knees buckle, but I don't fall. I can't.

I'm being held up...by Grim.

GRIM

"But, I saw you in the morgue. I kissed you. You were dead. You weren't breathing," Tricks says. She holds onto my arms, digging her trembling fingers into my skin as if she's afraid I'll fade into mist like a ghost if she lets go.

"I was breathing," I assure her. "Just barely. And I felt that kiss. I thought it was a dream." I push a strand of curls from her eyes and cup her cheek. She leans into my touch. "I'm alive. So are Sandy and Haze. So is Marci, as you can see, and Gabby's alive but hasn't woken up from surgery."

Tricks's exhale comes from the very depths of her

body, expelling the despair she'd been carrying around with her for who knows how long. She collapses against me. I lift her into my arms and carry her back out into Marci's room. She's still sleeping. I sit her down on the couch and take her hands in mine.

"With so many people after us, I couldn't get to you. But if they all thought we were dead, we'd be able to move around undetected, at least for a while. The chief's medicine woman gave us some root that's like morphine to put us into a deep sleep. Then, the coroner tossed us in the fridge to lower our body temperature. The second Lemming left, they gave us a shot of adrenaline to wake us up. We were heading back to the reservation to see if chief David found out where they were keeping you when we came across the overturned car. At first, I thought you..."

"It doesn't feel good, does it?" she asks, drying her tears with the back of her hand.

"No, it fucking does not."

She presses her lips together. "The shooters! Shit, do you think they could identify you? It could blow your entire plan."

"They could," I respond. "If they were still alive."

She exhales. "Good."

"I'm so sorry, Tricks. I wanted Lemming to see us for confirmation. Not you. I never thought he would take you there."

"It's not your fault. And it's a smart plan...except... Lemming isn't Lemming."

"What does that mean?" I hold her face still in my hands.

"He's Callum Egan."

SEVEN

"IT WAS PROBABLY HIS MEN SHOOTING AT ME WHEN I escaped to drive back here," I say to Grim.

He presses his forehead to mine. "They weren't Irish. We saw them. They were Marco's men."

"I'm so confused," I groan.

"Gabby's awake," Sandy says, poking his head through the door. "She wants to see you."

Grim helps me to my feet. "You're exhausted, you should rest. We'll talk more later."

I shake my head. "I have to see Gabby."

Grim never let's go of my arm as he guides me down the hall to Gabby's room.

I'm surprised to see Gabby sitting up when I arrive. Sandy, Haze, and Grim keep to the wall by the door as a nurse excuses herself.

I run to the bed and stop short of flinging myself at Gabby. "You're okay!" I exclaim.

Both her eyes and her smile are bright. "I'm tougher than I look. The doctors had to stitch up an artery. It wasn't severed, just nicked. I could've bled to death if Grim hadn't brought me here when he did."

"But, you didn't," I whisper. "And he did."

She grabs my hand. "But, I didn't. And he did."

I sit at the edge of the bed. "You certainly are tougher than you look. Did you really kill Gil?"

She nods and looks nothing short of proud. "I went to find you the night of the funeral. I had a bad feeling. I overheard Marco talking about something big going down with Bedlam that night. I didn't want you to be caught up in it. I didn't see you there. I remember you saying Grim had a room in the back. The door was unlocked. Gil was inside rummaging through things. He had a huge knife in his hands he'd just pulled from a drawer. I went to run from the room to go warn you but he pulled me back in. During the struggle, we both fell. He dropped the knife. I grabbed it, and he wrapped his hands around my throat and pulled me up to the bed. I was seeing stars but pretended to be passed out or dead, or I don't know, but he fell for it. The second he released me, I grabbed the knife from the mattress and...well... you know. I stabbed him."

"In the fucking head. Quite impressive strength,"

Sandy says from the doorway, looking more than impressed. He winks.

Gabby blushes. "I didn't mean to stab him in the head. Or, I should say I wasn't aiming for anything in particular, just him in general. It's just where the knife landed."

"Leave it where it lies," Sandy says, leaning his elbows on the mattress.

"Isn't that a golf thing?" Haze asks.

Sandy shrugs. "Sure, but right now it's a stabbing in the head thing."

Gabby smiles, but it quickly drops from her face as she turns her attention back to me. "There was something else Marco said. She looks around to each of us, then settles on me. EJ, Marco.... he murdered Belly."

Haze growls. "We know. He was poisoned, but how?"

"The whiskey," Gabby said. "He was poisoning Belly's whiskey. Something about the special stuff he kept in the garage."

"Shit," Sandy swears, rubbing his temples.

"But, how did he get to the whiskey in the garage?" Sandy asks.

"He got to it before it got to the garage," Gabby explains. "The guy at the liquor store. He was in on it. Marco must have paid him off. I'm so sorry. All of this is because of my own flesh and blood." She wrings her hands on her lap.

Sandy sits on the other side of Gabby's bed. "As far as we are concerned, you're Tricks's sister. No relation to Marco or Mona."

"Mona?" Gabby asks with a gasp. "What about her?"

Sandy grimaces. "Shit, you didn't know about that one did you."

"Dumbass," Haze mutters. Sandy backhands his chest.

I take a deep breath. "Mona did some horrible things. She's been working with Marco." Gabby remains silent as I fill her in on the rest of what her sister's done.

"I can't believe she's been here all this time and never told me. And that she is capable…that doesn't sound like the Mona I knew."

"It doesn't. I couldn't believe it either. But, that Mona we knew? She doesn't exist anymore."

"I'm so sorry, EJ," Gabby sobs.

I hug her tightly around her shoulders, pulling her into my chest. I kiss her hair. "Stop apologizing. It's not your fault. I don't blame you for any of this."

"But— "

"Gabriella Ramos," I blurt. I take her face in my hands and stare deeply into her huge dark eyes. "Love means never having to say you're sorry."

Her lips turn upward slightly. She sniffles. "Erich Segal, American writer."

"Nailed it," I chuckle. "But, seriously. Promise me, right here and right now, that you're done apologizing. I'm tired of hearing it and thinking it. There's nothing for you to be sorry about. *Nothing*. Now, promise me."

"I'll try," Gabby says with a small nod.

"You know what they say about trying?" I return her smile and wipe the tears off her cheek with my thumb.

"Things don't always work the first time, but keep trying," she answers.

"And who— "I start to ask.

"Donald Duck."

All heads swing to a smug-looking Sandy.

Gabby wrinkles her nose. "How did you know that?"

He shrugs and flashes her a megawatt grin.

"Don't let the idiot fool you," Grim warns Gabby. "He's kind of a genius."

"Where is Mona now?" Gabby asks.

"I don't know." I answer honestly.

"Uhhh…" Sandy starts, biting his lip. He slowly raises his hand. "I know."

"You do?" Gabby and I ask at the same time.

I lean across the bed to Sandy. "Where?"

Grim speaks for the first time since we arrived in Gabby's room. "She's here."

EIGHT

"IS THIS WHAT YOU REALLY WANT TO DO?" I ASK
Tricks as we walk from the reservation hospital to the
war room.

"I don't want to. I have to," she corrects.

"She showed up here at the hospital only a few
minutes after I brought Gabby in. She seemed apolo-
getic. I don't know if it's bullshit or if she's telling the
truth." We stop at the door to the war room, and I turn
Tricks to face me. "Look at me."

She does, but her face is unreadable. She looks lost in
thought. "What you have to ask yourself right now,
before you go in there, is this: does it make a difference
to you if Mona's truly sorry? Will it change what you
want the outcome to be?"

"Does it matter what I decide?"

I shake my head. "Not to me. It has to matter to you. You have to know what you want to get out of this before you take a step inside that door. Whether it's revenge, or salvation. Trust me, it makes all the difference to how you will feel when you walk back out."

She looks at the door and then back to me. "Okay. I'm ready."

"Just like that?" I ask.

"Just like that," she repeats, looking to the door.

I open it and follow her inside. Rollo is perched at the edge of the table, reading a book.

"You know how to read?" I tease.

"Don't be jealous. Wuthering Heights is the greatest book of all time."

I raise my eyebrows and wait for him to finish.

Rollo closes the book and sets it on the table. "Or so Trinity's Tinder profile states. It also says she used to be a gymnast and can tie her legs behind her head like a pretzel."

"And the truth comes out."

"Why, hello there, Mrs. Grim Reaper," he says to Tricks, adding a dramatic bow.

She offers Rollo a smile. "Hi, I'm Emma Jean Parish," she introduces, reminding me of the first time we met.

Rollo bites his lip, looking at her in a way that makes me want to punch him in the face. She holds out her hand to shake, but the motherfucker picks her up and embraces her in a tight hug. "I'm glad to see you're okay. Grim had us worried about you for a while. You should have seen him. He was freaking the fuck—"

"Put her down," I growl.

Rollo places her back on the floor and raises his hands. "Just being friendly with the queen of Bedlam is all, Boss" he says, flashing her a wink.

My murderous thoughts fade as he steps aside to reveal Mona, sitting at the long end of the table, her wrists bound to the chair.

Tricks freezes.

I lean down and whisper in her ear. "You don't have to say anything to her. We can leave if you want."

She shakes her head and takes a deep breath. "No, I need to say something to her."

I stand back as Tricks walks to Mona, pulls out the chair and takes a seat next to her. She, then, yanks on Mona's chair, forcing Mona to face her.

"Knife," she demands holding up her hand.

I remove my blade from the sheath under my pant leg and walk over to her, setting it in Tricks's outstretched hand.

"Thank you, my love," she says, never taking her eyes off Mona as she closes her hand around the handle of the blade.

My love. Those two words make my heart stutter like

I've stuck my finger in an electric socket. It forces me to cough into my fist. Tricks looks over her shoulder to make sure I'm okay. I give her the nod. She turns back around to face Mona. Making a show of spinning the blade around her hand, catching the fluorescent light above.

"You're like a love-sick school boy, ain't ya, Boss?" Rollo whispers. He's standing next to me against the wall, watching Tricks in action. He continues, "I can see why. Beautiful, cool as fuck, puts up with your shit. Likes knives."

Tricks holds up the blade and leans in toward her former friend. With her free hand, she rips the gag from Mona's mouth.

My stuttering chest swells with pride.

"Shut the fuck up, or I'll use that blade on you when she's done with it," I hiss.

"Fair enough." Rollo waits three seconds before elbowing me in the ribs. "Boss? Uh…what do you think your ole lady is gonna to do with that blade?"

I watch as the fear grows in Mona's eyes. Her mouth falls open.

"Honestly?" I ask. "I have no fucking idea." We both watch as Tricks twirls the handle of the knife on Mona's knee, toying with her fear. "But, I can't wait to find out."

"EJ, I'm so sorry. I'm so fucking sorry," Mona says,

her face pales. "I have no excuse. I had nothing, no one. Just like you."

Tricks scoffs. "You had nothing, just like I had nothing?" she repeats Mona's words as a question. I can't take my eyes off her. She's always been the most beautiful girl in the world, but right now, with her taking control of the situation, showing her strength with every movement, she's living, breathing sex.

I adjust my position against the wall in an attempt to make my raging cock heel.

"Let's get something straight right the fuck now, Mona. You went to Los Muertos *willingly* to help Marco hurt me. You bought into his lies. Gabby and I were taken there as kids and threatened every day with death or being sold on the streets. We weren't allowed to go to school. We weren't allowed to talk to anyone. We were wiped from the system like we didn't exist and then treated like we didn't exist. We weren't kids or even people. We were dogs. And when we wouldn't heel, they brought you in, and it makes sense. You already hated me. It couldn't have been too hard to turn you against me."

"I never hated you. I just hated the way I felt. Like you and Gabby were sisters, and I was the outsider. Please, let me see her."

"I'm not letting you anywhere near her until she tells me she wants to see you. You felt like an outsider because you made yourself an outsider. We never excluded you. You just refused to join us. And on the rare occasion you did, you brought your misery with you." I shake my head. "I'm not going to apologize to you. We were kids, Mona. Kids. We all had fucked up childhoods. You want to know what the real difference is between me and you?"

"No," she shakes her head.

"You've let the past consume you while I won't let it define who I am."

Mona shuts her eyes. "I know."

"We were all victims." Tricks says. "I just never thought, in a million years, I'd be your victim."

Tricks stabs the knife into the table.

Mona continues on a shaky voice. "I didn't know I was capable of such...horrible things. But every time I did them, Marco praised me. For studying psychology, I was so easily duped into becoming a weapon for my brother to wield as he saw fit." Mona's bottom lip quivers. "I let my jealousy cloud everything and my want for a family fuck up everything. I trusted my brother when I should have trusted you and Gabby." She lowers her voice to a whisper. "I love you, you know. I always have. You and Gabriella. I may have lost my way for a while, but I know now. You two are everything to me."

Tricks pulls the blade from the wood and leans over

Mona. "No," she hisses. "We *were* everything to you. We're dead to you now, just like you planned."

"No!" Mona begins to argue. Tricks shoves the gag back into her mouth and walks up to where Rollo and I are standing against the wall. I wish we were alone. Naked. I want to worship every part of her like the queen she is.

We stare at each other. The connection between us explodes like a transformer on a utility pole.

Rollo clears his throat. "What do you want me to do with her?'" He glances over at Mona.

I look to Tricks. "It's your call."

She thinks for a moment, pulling her bottom lip between her teeth. "I'll talk to Gabby. We'll decide together."

I nod. "Rollo, stay with her for now. Don't let the bitch out of your sight."

"Mmmffffffffffmmmmmm," Mona cries from behind her gag.

Tricks spares Mona one last glance before we walk to the door.

"Whether you live or die."

NINE

I DON'T REMEMBER GOING TO SLEEP. ONCE MY exhaustion took hold, I was done for. I wake wearing nothing but a Bedlam Brotherhood t-shirt. I look around for Grim, but he's not around. There's a note on the pillow beside me in the indent where he'd slept.

66 Mastering others is strength. Mastering yourself is true power."

– LAO TZU

I grin at Grim's use of the quote and hold the note to my chest.

"It's true, you know," Grim says, his massive body taking up every inch of the doorway. His jeans are slung low. He's shirtless as usual but devoid of the hooded jacket. "I've never known anyone like you. Beautiful. Smart. Cunning. Strong. I've never been proud of anyone before. But last night…I was so fucking proud of you. You are powerful beyond measure." He stalks toward the bed. His lean muscles flex under his beautifully tattooed skin.

He pulls me into a sitting position and tangles his fingers in my hair. His lips barely touch mine in a teasing kiss, and I moan at the contact, but I quickly pull away.

"What's wrong?" he asks, breathing hard.

I cover my mouth and mumble behind my hand. "I haven't brushed my teeth yet."

He laughs and lifts me from the bed. "Then, to the shower we go." He takes a step, then winces.

"What's wrong?"

"Ah, it's nothing," he says. The wince is gone, but he's got a slight limp I hadn't noticed the night before.

"No, it's not nothing. What the fuck happened?"

"I was shot."

I gasp, remembering one of the task force agents, or Callum's men, or whoever they were, saying that Grim was shot, but after thinking him dead then seeing him alive and well again, the bullet he might have taken slipped my mind.

Grim has the audacity to chuckle at my concern. I

place my hand on my hip flash him my best disapproving look.

He grabs me by the shoulders. "It was only in the leg, baby. The bullet's out. It's barely a scrape. I've been hurt worse."

I try to ignore the tingling sensation between my legs and my hardening nipples at his calling me baby. "You've been—"

"Hey guys," Sandy says, popping his head in. "I'm switching places with Rollo for a while. Question, do I bring food out to the chick, or are we starving her out?" he asks. It's a very matter of fact question. "Yes? No?"

This is Bedlam, I think to myself. Business as usual. It's probably not the first time Sandy's asked that question. It might not be the last.

"Feed her," Grim orders. "I want her coherent."

Grim looks to me and explains further. "Gabby's been asking to see Mona all morning. Figured she'll want to confront her sister and hear her side. She can't talk if she's passed out from hunger."

I nod.

"And Marci's up and about," Sandy adds. "She wants to leave the hospital against the doctors' orders. I'm about to head up there."

"Shit," Grim says, rubbing his palm over his stubble which is much longer than I'm used to seeing on him. "I'll go with you." He grabs his jacket from the table and plants a kiss on top of my head. "Shower. Eat. I'll be back soon, and then, I'm taking you somewhere. There's a team our guys surrounding the place. Haze is in the hall."

"That I am!" Haze calls out. "Your Bedlam body-guard at your service, madam."

"I'll meet you in Marci's room," Sandy says to Grim. "I gotta do something first."

"Like what?" Grim asks.

Sandy looks to the wall above our heads as he speaks. "Uhhh, I'm... you know...just going to check in on Gabby." He drums his fingers against his thighs. "You know, just to make sure she doesn't need anything." He darts off.

"That was odd," I comment, looking at the empty spot in the doorway Sandy just vacated.

Grim shrugs. "That was *Sandy*."

"You think he has the hots for Gabby?"

"I know he does. Her and every other pretty girl within a twenty-mile radius."

"Fifty, at least," Haze corrects from the hall.

Grim shrugs on his jacket.

"Good luck talking Marci out of leaving," I say, running my hands over the heat of his chest.

He shakes his head. "I'm not going to tell her she should stay. Once Marci makes up her mind, the decision is made. There's no point in arguing."

"Then, why *are* you going?" I ask, knitting my eyebrows.

Grim plants a quick kiss to my lips. "To make sure she doesn't take out any of the nurses or burn the damn building down on her way out."

Grim

Marci is dressed in her regular clothes when Sandy and I arrive at her room after he spent a good amount of time talking quietly about god only knows what with Gabby in hers.

"I assume you two are here to escort me out, so I don't make a scene," Marci says.

"The four of us actually," Tricks answers, entering the room with Haze.

"Sorry, I couldn't stop her," Haze says.

Tricks looks up at me apologetically. Her hair is wet from what had to be the world's quickest shower. I hope she, at least, ate something and remind myself to ask her when we're done at the hospital.

"She's not a prisoner," I say. "She can go wherever she wants." I take her hand in mine.

"Damn right, she's not. She's family," Marci says. "Boys?" she asks Sandy and Haze. "Will you go get me the release forms the doctors are taking their sweet time with?'

Haze and Sandy leave the room.

I pull Tricks over to the couch. She takes a seat while I help Marci tie the laces on her boots.

"Thank you, my sweet boy."

I tie the last knot as a shadow crosses the doorway.

I reach for my gun and stand. I turn around just as Agent Lemming steps from the shadows.

Marci's eyes go wide. "Callum?"

I don't even have time to be shocked that the son of a bitch has the balls to step foot onto the reservation and into Bedlam territory after trying to kidnap Tricks.

Before Callum can breathe a word, my gun is aimed and cocked at his head. I'm seething with hatred, and if my girl wasn't standing in the room, this fucker's brains would be sliding down the wall behind him.

Marci shuffles over to Tricks, keeping her protectively behind her.

"I had a feeling it was all a ruse," Callum says, his lips curving up at the corners. "Good to see you back in the land of the living."

I hold my gun steady. "Thanks, I intend to stay awhile, in case you had other plans."

He raises his hands, slowly from his sides. He's holding something. It's not a weapon, but a white handkerchief. He dangles it, holding just a corner. He waves it around. "I come in peace. I'm not armed. I'm just here to talk."

"So, talk." I say, not lowering my gun.

He leans to the side, looking over my shoulder. "I'm here about the girl."

"Like hell you are," I say. There's no fucking way I'm allowing him anywhere near Tricks since he'd tried to load her onto a plane and take her to fuck knows where.

"Why? Who is she to you?" Marci asks.

Callum straightens. "She's my daughter." "Bullshit! Why should I fucking believe you?" I ask, holding both my words and my gun steady.

"I can prove it. Just let me talk to her," Callum says, his accent thick and Irish.

I shake my head. "You'll talk to me first before I let you anywhere near her."

"Very well then. By all means. Let us talk." Callum produces an envelope from his pocket. "And while we talk —." He looks to Tricks once more. "I'd like her to read these. They're just letters. They ain't gonna kill her," he says when I eye them suspiciously.

Tricks is now behind me. She reaches under my arm and grabs the letters.

Callum confidently looks to her, then me. "I'm all yours. Lead the way."

TEN

I TAKE CALLUM TO THE MAIN LIVING AREA ATTACHED to the brothel. Callum takes a seat. I sit beside him at the head of the table, resting my gun on my lap and my hand on my gun.

"You know by now that it wasn't Bedlam who took your shipment," I tell him.

"I do know that, but it's not why I'm here. I'm here about my daughter."

"And how exactly are you so sure that she's your daughter?" I ask skeptically. "There seems to be another hat in the ring for that title."

"That's absurd," he laughs.

"You should take a walk in my shoes. You have no fucking idea what absurd is. You want to talk to my girl?

Well, I want answers. One doesn't happen without the other. So, if I were you, I'd start talking."

Callum sighs and pushes a photograph across the table. It's of a younger Callum, a woman with honey blonde curls like Tricks, and a baby girl sitting between them. "That's my family before my baby girl was ripped away from me and her mother. She's mine. I've been looking for her since she was a babe, and now, I've found her. You want proof?" He claps his hands together. "Fine. I'll submit to any and all blood tests. Whatever you've got. I'm as sure she's mine as the days are long."

"We'll see about that," I say.

Callum sighs. "I'll tell you how it all started, but I'd rather have her here —"

Our heads snap to the door where a pale-faced Tricks appears. She's holding the letters Callum had given her in her shaky hand. "I don't..." she starts then pauses to collect herself. She holds up the letters. "Is this all true?"

"Aye, every word," Callum responds.

I stand and pull out a chair for Trick's guiding her to sit. She passes me the letters.

Callum points to the one with feminine handwriting. "This one first."

Dearest Fernando,
At one time you were my greatest love, and now you're my biggest regret.

The child I'm carrying isn't yours, but you're not a stupid man, I have no doubt you know this by now. I'm writing this because I need you to know that's not the reason I'm suddenly gone from Los Muertos and from your life.

I took Gabriella and Mona, my daughter and yours, because they don't deserve to grow up in that hellish place. I couldn't live with myself anymore, knowing their lives would always be in jeopardy in one way or another. That they wouldn't ever get to be kids. Carefree. Without violence. I want them to be loved. To be part of a family. A real family.

I won't let what happened to Marco happen to them. I saw the devil in his eyes last night as he sat at the table twirling a knife into the wood. My plan was to take him, too, but there's no saving him now. He's killed for the first time, and the blood of the poor boy who found himself on the receiving end of Marco's wrath, has twisted his mind and corroded his soul.

I can't save Marco, but I can save the girls. I will save the girls. Then, there was Emma Jean. I knew better than to ask questions about where she came from or why you'd brought her to Los Muertos. What you don't know is that I spent most of the night vomiting, and not because of the child in my belly, but from disgust. God only knows whose hands she was ripped from, or what fate she would suffer at your own. I tried to tell myself she was a bastard child of yours, and that maybe, you were doing the right thing by bringing her home to raise her yourself. But, there is not a drop of your blood in that beautiful pale-faced gringa. I know because I searched for it over and over again. I won't allow

63

*this child to be a tool in your already cluttered work box or as a
pawn in the game of life and death you play so well.*

*In the end, it doesn't matter who she is. All that matters is that
she isn't there with you.*

*As much as I wish to raise the girls myself, I know it's not possi-
ble. In time, you'll catch up to me and you'll kill me for all I've
done. For the evidence I handed over to the FEDS that has landed
you in prison. When you do, you should know the girls won't be
with me. They'll be somewhere else. Somewhere safe.*

I have made many, many mistakes in my life, Fernando.

This is not one of them.

When I die, they will live on.

*I'm not asking you to spare my life, but I am asking you to spare
the lives of Mona, Gabriella, and Emma Jean. If you have any
ounce of humanity left in you, please, don't look for them. Don't
bring them back to that place. If you love your daughters at all,
and if you ever truly loved me, then please, let them go.*

Yours,

Camilla

Intrigued and baffled, I flip to the next letter,
surprised to find it's actually from Fernando himself.

My Dearest Camilla,

*I'm writing this letter to you from prison, but you knew that's
where I'd end up because you're the one who became una rata and
handed over enough evidence to the FEDS to send and keep me*

here for a minimum of fifty years to life. By my count, I've got forty-six more to go. Although, I won't make it that long. I'm afraid I won't even make it through the month. So, life it is. I'm sick. Very sick. Which is probably why I'm writing this letter to you now after all this time, knowing you'll never read it. I'm a coward like that. I always have been. At least when it came to you. You see, the cancer has spread to my brain, amongst other vital organs — like my heart — which the prison doctor assures me I do have, despite your past accusations to the contrary.

You were right, mi amor. About so many things. I did come for you, just like you said I would, and I did find you…and, well you know the rest.

I would tell you that I'm sorry, but apologizing to the dead is like whispering in a deaf man's ear.

Pointless.

I admit I did what you asked me not to do. I located the girls. It was clever how you put Gabriella and Mona in one foster home and Emma Jean in another. You knew I'd be looking for three girls together. I also like the last name you gave Emma Jean. Parish. Your mother's maiden name. Cute. It was also clever how you were able to have their records sealed. No doubt due to the deal you'd struck with the FEDS in return for my head on a platter. It's too late now, but you should have demanded witness protection as well.

I really wish you had.

Back to the girls. Clever or not, it only took one phone call and I had all three of their files in my hands, addresses and all.

I was arrested before I had the chance to retrieve them and bring them back. I did have plans for Emma Jean. To use her in a way that would benefit Los Muertos. I was going to have Marco carry out my plan, but then, something happened. It was Marco. He came to the prison with a file I'd asked him to bring. Power of attorney documents, and other boring paperwork that needed to be taken care of so Marco could take officially take the reins and become the leader of Los Muertos.

But then something fell out of the documents as I was signing them. It was a sealed envelope. A letter. Your letter. Written on the day you ran off. It must have fallen from the table or been pushed into the drawer with the file.

My deepest regret was and still is having read it three months too late.

As if I was making up for not reading it then, I read it a hundred times a day during the weeks leading up to my sentencing and several times a day still.

It was your letter that opened my eyes. So much so that when Marco came to see me again. I was finally able to see the devil in his eyes, as you so eloquently put it. He never even asked about his sisters. Not once. It's like they never existed at all in his mind. It's all my fault that he's become a blood-thirsty power-hungry monster. I raised a soldier, not a son. Even as a young child, when his mother had just died soon after giving birth to Mona, he didn't shed one single tear. I didn't recollect that until now. I didn't see or didn't care what I was doing to my own boy, and you're right. It's too late for him.

But it's not too late for me. Not my body, that's clearly on the way out. And not my soul, I pissed-out that withered up thing long ago. But since you can't apologize to the dead, I can at least respect the dead's final wishes.

I never told Marco about my plans for Emma Jean. Instead, I let the girls be. That is, until very recently, when I arranged for Emma Jean to be placed in the same home as Gabriella and Mona in hopes the three of them will grow up and navigate this lonesome world together. I can't give them the family you wanted them to have, but I can give them each other. If I could, I'd send Emma Jean back to where she came from, or rather, where I'd taken her from, but it's too late now. It would only bring about more harm and pain when my intention is, for the first time, to bring about less.

Several times a day, I start writing letters to Mona and Gabriella. Every single one winds up in a crumpled ball beneath my mattress. I know I'm poison, and would be so even from behind cell bars. I don't want them to get to know the dying man version of me, and I don't want them to know the man I was. I know this letter is growing long and dull, but I only have a few things left to say to you. The first, is that I forgive you for finding comfort with the chief when I offered you none in the life I was supposed to share with you, not make you fearful of. And I'm not really forgiving you, because you have nothing to be sorry for. I'm the one who needs forgiveness, for taking your life and the life of your unborn child, but as I've said, I'm not seeking it.

The second thing I want to tell you is about the girl you call

Emma Jean, which I've now taken to thinking of her as myself. I must have been muttering when I brought her to Los Muertos that night. You always said I was not much of a talker and more of a mutterer. And, Camilla, I'm only telling you this because it's not possible for you to ever tell another living soul. You didn't get a chance to take this secret to the grave, but I'm taking it to mine.

Her name isn't Emma Jean.

Her name is Imogen.

Imogen Egan.

The daughter of Callum Egan.

I won't see you in this life or the next. I'm pretty sure there are no elevators up for visits, and if there are, I'm pretty sure you'd be smart enough to refuse me. So, I will simply say this: goodbye, mi amor. And even though you can't apologize to the dead, for what it's worth, and I know it's not much, I'm so very sorry.

Yours Forever,

Fernando

ELEVEN

WHILE GRIM FINISHES READING THE LETTERS I JUST
can't wrap my head around it all. Callum, however,
remains unfazed, singing under his breath.

"Too-ra-loo-ra-loo-ral
Too-ra-loo-ra-li
Too-ra-loo-ra-loo-ral
Hush now, don't you cry
Too-ra-loo-ra-loo-ral
Too-ra-loo-ra-li
Too-ra-loo-ra-loo-ral"

"That song," I say, "I hear that song in my head.
Always have. What is it?"

Callum stops singing. "It's an old Irish folk song.

Catchy isn't it? I used to sing it to you as a babe to get you to go to sleep. Worked every time. It's the only thing that did. You were a stubborn little thing."

I'm silent as I take in his words. "Could it be really be true? Everything in the letters?"

"You could be his daughter," Grim answers the question I didn't think I asked out loud. He sets down the letters. "Or, you could be Chief David's."

Grim fills me and Callum in on his theory about Marco and the reason for the marriage Marco insisted on. Some of it makes sense, and some of it doesn't. Why would Marco risk my life so many times if I was so valuable to him? My head feels like a pinball machine. Except in my game, the glass is broken, and the pinballs are bouncing wildly all over the floor.

I'm exhausted. Confused. Grim senses my troubles and places a hand on my knee to steady me.

"We were at home, in Ireland. You were but a wee thing. Your mother and I, well, we never thought we could have children of our own, then you came along. You were, *are*, very special to us. Our miracle, if you believe in such things. One night, we sang you to sleep like we usually did. Your mother and I drifted off shortly after, knowing you were right next to our bed in your cradle, same as you'd been every night since the day you came screaming into the world."

He stares at the ceiling as he recalls the memory, then looks to his lap. He frowns at his hands.

"The next morning, when we woke, my guards were all dead and Aileen, your ma, is screaming bloody murder." He looks to me. "'Cause you're gone." His fists clench, his words are strained. "We looked high and low for you. Never stopped. I know that this business of mine comes with a price, but there are rules about family. I looked everywhere, to both my enemies and my friends. I had eyes on every organization in six countries, but there was no sign of you anywhere. It was almost like you'd never been born at all. Months passed, then years. But we never stopped looking. Not for one single second."

Callum reaches into his jacket pocket and slides me a crinkled photograph. It's a younger version of him standing next to a much shorter woman with the same honey colored curls as my own. In her arms is a laughing baby, frozen mid-clap.

He points to the baby. "That's you, me, and that there, is your ma, Aileen."

My *mother.* I rub my thumb over her smile. My heart thumps in my chest as if remembering how to beat. I inhale and exhale sharply. My chest feels weighted, yet lighter. If this is my mother, then why isn't she here? A thought occurs to me.

"Is she…" I begin to ask.

Callum cuts me off. "No, no. She's not dead. She's fit as a fiddle. Waiting for you, very impatiently, I might add, back in Ireland. It took a whole lot of convincing to make her stay put. If she had her way, she'd been dressed in one of the task force vests and helmets, storming Los Muertos like a single woman herd of wild horses." He claps his hands together and sets them on the table. "A mother's love knows no boundaries. No laws. Neither does a fathers."

"How...how did you find me? Why now? After all this time?" I ask without taking my eyes off the woman who is, without a doubt, my mother. "It doesn't make any sense. Marco apparently thinks that I'm the chiefs daughter. He even married me so he could extract bene-fits from the tribe."

Callum chuckles. "Marco's an idjiot of the highest degree. A soon to be dead idjiot at that. You see, when his father Fernando died in prison, he died with a secret he never planned on telling a soul." He reaches under the seat and hands me an envelope with two crumbled letters inside. "Except, in the end, he did. A guard recently found those behind a loose brick in a cell in the State Penitentiary."

"And he contacted you instead of handing it over to the proper authorities?" I raise my eyebrow.

Callum shrugs. "The proper authorities don't pay as well as I do."

My mind wanders back to the letters. "Marco

assumed I was Camilla and the chief's daughter..." I think out loud.

"If he did, it makes sense. The three of you were together when he found you in the foster home. Camila had taken you all at the same time. I can see how he could make that assumption," Callum admits. "You know, the first time I saw you I didn't even know it was you." He shakes his head and looks to his hands. "Didn't even recognize my own daughter. You were in the park, being roughed up by Mal. In all fairness your hair was different then. Straight and much darker. I saw your yellow shoes from afar. I may not have known who you were, but maybe my subconscious knew, because all I could think about was getting that bastards hands off ya."

He's talking about the day in the park. Around the time I discovered that Grim was Tristan Paine, the boy from my past.

Grim leans forward. "It was you, wasn't it, Callum? You're the one who shot into the crowd," he accuses.

Callum's forehead wrinkles as he considers his reply. "Yes...and no. Despite what's said about me, about who I am and what I've done, I'm not a wolf in the woods. My decisions, my actions, they are carefully calculated. The code I live by may not be up to church standards, but I don't go about killing women and children or shooting into crowds like some lowbrow hoodlum. Aye, I pulled the trigger that day, warning shots, nothing more...and they worked." He sighs. "Mal let you go. Then, when the crowd scattered, I lost sight of ya. Didn't see you again until the surveillance video at the marina stadium."

"The what?" I ask, an uneasy feeling burning in my chest. The video? Of the night Grim and I... I feel my face blanch as all the color rushes to my quick beating heart.

Grim answers before Callum can. "The marina surveillance video. The night of Belly's funeral. He showed me pictures at the station, of me *kissing* you." There's an ever so slight emphasis on the word kissing which leads me to believe that's all Callum saw. Grim's words douse the uneasy feeling. Inwardly I sigh in relief as the color returns to my face.

"Aye, and I told him then that I knew it wasn't just a kiss," Callum adds. "I know love when I see it. I remember what it was like when I first met my Aileen." He looks to the ceiling as if he's watching the memory playing out above his head. "I imagine we looked a lot like the two of you did in that video."

A realization crashes into me. "So, you knew who I was, and you knew there was something between Grim and myself. You knew he wasn't responsible for abducting me, yet you still ordered your men to shoot to kill him when you stormed the compound." It wasn't a question, it was an outright accusation.

Callum doesn't bother denying it or apologizing. "I did, but just like there is no real Agent Lemming, there is no real Task Force either. Those were my men, Clan Egan men, and they already had orders not to shoot Grim, well, not to kill anyway, since I suspected he might beat me in getting to you. Smoke and mirrors and all that."

He spreads his fingers and, with open palms, circles the air before him much like a magician after a magic trick. He shakes his head and smiles.

"I may not have recognized you the first time in the park, but I knew it was you in that video. My heart leapt from my chest and splattered out before me. My Imogen, right there in front of my eyes, for the first time since you were a babe." His wags his pointer finger at my hair. "Those curls of yours—your mother's curls—they don't lie. Even in black and white."

Hearing him even speak of my mother makes me feel like the room around us is spinning. With each rotation I grow more and more confused about what I should think. How I'm supposed to feel. I don't even know what that should be. Am I happy to discover who my parents could possibly be? Am I upset that my father isn't the straight-laced accountant type I always imagined he was?

I feel numb.

"What do you want from me?" I ask, my voice so low it's barely audible.

His lips flatten, his words sincere. "To be your father. A family. That's all. Truly."

The numbness is short-lived. All at once, a thousand different emotions collide into me like a raging bull, knocking me off my center. My head spins. It's all too much. "It's all too much," I repeat my words out loud as I push back the chair. "I...I have to go. To get out of here. I need to be somewhere else. Anywhere else."

My chair scrapes backward, and I make a run for the door. Yanking it open, I run as fast as I can, down the hall and away from that room. Away from the confusion. Away from the life-changing conversation. Away from Callum.

Away from my *father*.

TWELVE

I MAKE A MOVE TO FOLLOW TRICKS, BUT CALLUM stops me. "Let her have a moment alone. It's a lot to take in, and there's more to discuss."

As much as it pains me not to follow her, Callum is right. She needs time to process. I sit back down.

Callum rubs his eyes, and I realize how tired he looks. Not as if he needs a nap, but weary, the kind of tired you feel after years of struggles, not after missing a few hours of sleep. "In hindsight, I should have taken Marco out right then and there. But Imogen was the priority and nothing else. When I go, I'll leave you with a dozen of my men to help you finish the task with Marco. Win this war, Grim. Take back your city."

"I appreciate that, but honestly, I'm surprised that you won't want to stay and help take Marco out."

"There was once a time I'd been so bloodthirsty to take out a man who's done harm to my family that I'd have slaughtered an entire flock of sheep, looking for the wolf hiding among them. I'm not that man anymore. I've learned over time what's important, and that's why I must go and leave you the honor of killing the wolf."

"Where will you go?" I ask.

"Home. To Ireland." He leans over the table. "But first, I want to talk to you about Imogen."

I know what's coming. I deflect, as if putting off his words could stop her from leaving. "Are we about to have the *stay away from my daughter* talk?"

Callum laughs. "Not exactly. I don't want you to necessarily stay away from her, but it's not like it will be safe for her here while you are fighting this war."

He's right. "It won't be."

"I'd like to take Imogen home to Ireland with me."

"Isn't that up to her?" I cross my arms over my chest.

"It is up to her. I'm just hoping you won't be standing in the way of her making that decision."

"I wouldn't do that." As much as the thought of her leaving pains me, Egan is right. It's not safe. "I'd already suggested sending her away before. It didn't go over well." Although, I wouldn't be sending her away this time. She'd be going toward something. A real home. Family. "I'll try and make her understand."

"Good. Because Imogen's mother is eagerly awaiting

the arrival of her long-lost daughter. She'll already be wondering why we were delayed. I don't want to find out what happens to me if I step off that plane without Imogen."

He chuckles, then takes out his phone and presses a few buttons.

"What are you doing?"

"Calling in reinforcements," he says. "In case you decide to change your mind and stand in the way of Imogen's decision to come home with me."

I'm about to ask him what the hell he means by *reinforcements* when he passes me the phone. A woman with Tricks's curls, the same woman from the picture appears on the screen. She's Tricks in every way, but older, with tiny lines around her eyes.

"Callum is that you? Did you find her? Does she know who you are? Let me see her!" she says, sounding equal parts panicked and excited. My image must appear on her screen. "Oh, you're not Callum." Her eyes widen. "Is he alright? Where is he?"

"I'm right here, love," Callum calls out.

She sighs with relief.

"I assume you must be Grim," she says with a smile. "My daughter's beau."

"I am, ma'am. And I assume you're Callum's reinforcements."

"No, don't you be calling me, ma'am. I'm barely forty

79

years old." She laughs. "And reinforcements?" She twists her lips. "Is that what he's calling his wife these days?"

Callum's shoulders shake with silent laughter.

"Grim, my boy, is she alright?" she asks. Her forehead wrinkles with concern.

"She's fine," I reassure her. "She's been through hell and back, but she'll be okay."

Tears spill from her eyes. Her head bobs in a continuous nod. "Good. Good. That's so very good."

"She knows now. Callum told her everything. She's read the letters."

"And?" she asks.

"And she needs some time alone."

"I bet she does. It's not every day you learn about your family. This all must be quite a shock to you and her both."

Everyday has been one shock after another.

"I can't wait to see her again. After all these years. To hold my girl in my arms." She's sobbing now, wiping her tears with a tissue. "I hope she'll like me." Her tears stop. Her eyes widen in shock. "Lord, what if she doesn't like me?"

I almost laugh at the ridiculous idea. "I don't like anyone, and yet, I find myself liking you already," I reassure her. "And Tricks...I mean Imogen. She's got a kind heart. A big one, too."

"That's so good to hear. I hope to see her soon. Give

her my love." She holds up the phone, and I realize she's in a room decorated all in pink. There's a crib in the corner. "Although, I'm thinking I'll have to redecorate. I don't think she'll fit in this wee crib."

She laughs, and I laugh right along with her although I realize Aileen is already assuming Tricks will go to Ireland. My heart lurches. I'm reminded of my own mother, of what I wouldn't give to see her again. To get to know her as an adult.

"I'm sure you have much to discuss with Callum, things much more important than interior decorating." She sniffles. "Give my girl my love, and Grim?"

"Yes?"

"Thank you for keeping her safe. For loving her during a time when she wasn't able to feel our love. It gives me great comfort, knowing she felt yours."

I don't know how to answer her. My throat tightens. I give her a simple nod in return.

Callum takes the phone. "I'll call you soon, my love," he says.

"Give my love to Marci," she replies.

Callum ends the call.

"Well played, Callum," I say leaning back in the chair.

He shrugs. "I've got to play every card I have."

"So, then this is all a game to you?"

His stare hardens. "No, it's not a game. It's my daughter, and you'll learn if you ever have children of your own that there ain't nothing a parent won't do for their kids. You think I'm capable of lies, deceit, and murder as head of Clan Egan?" He shakes his head and laughs. His voice deepens. "You have no idea what I'm capable of as a father."

I lean my elbows on the table. "If she does decide to go, you best keep her safe, Callum."

He raises his eyebrows in amusement. I don't trust him, even if the blood test proves Tricks is his daughter. Marco's living proof that being related by blood does not equal loyalty. "Is that a threat?"

I bore my words into his brain with an unblinking stare. "No. It's a fucking promise."

His smile turns flat. "I fucked it all up once, Grim. I won't be doing that again. She'll be safe. You have my word. I promise you that when all is said and done, and it's safe for her to return to Lacking--and she wishes to do so--I won't stop her. In fact, I'll bring her back myself."

"I appreciate that. But, there's more," I say.

"More than the threat of death?" Callum jokes.

"Not more from me. More for her. She's been a pris- oner. She's experienced so little in this life."

Understanding registers in Callum's eyes. "Aye. I've been waiting for many years to give Imogen the stars. She'll have her family. Free will. She'll have it all. She'll see things in Ireland she never knew existed. She'll have an education if she wants it. Tutors. Everything she missed out on and more. You have my word."

I search his face. I believe him. It's comforting and terrifying at the same time. "Plus, you have to take Gabriella."

"Marco's sister? Is she even alive? Last time I saw her, she was bleeding out."

"She's going to live," I tell him. "And she's blood related to Marco, but Gabby was raised as Tricks's sister, and just as much a prisoner. She's her closest friend, and up until now, her only real family."

"Why do you call her Tricks?" Callum asks.

I debate whether or not to tell him, but as I recall the story in my mind, I can't help but recite the day we met aloud.

"Now, she really reminds me of her mother. I can see why the Los Muertos girl is so important to her," Callum says. He thinks for a second, then shrugs. "My wife and I couldn't have any more children. Aileen will be over the moon if I come home with one daughter." He holds up two fingers. "Two? She might fall off the end of the Earth with joy."

"When are you planning on leaving?"

"The streets are already bloody and about to get bloodier. As soon as possible. Sooner, if she'll allow."

"I'll call the chief and see if we can expedite a DNA test."

"Aye, good plan. I'll talk to my men and ask the chief for a cabin to get some shut-eye."

Callum stands, but before he leaves, he pauses. "I know Imogen loves you, Grim. Any fool can see it in her eyes, and I know you love her as well. You hide your true self, but you can't hide that. It's written in your very soul and seeps out your pores. I know too much of the soul-sucking feeling that comes with having to live without her." He looks over his shoulder, and his eyes lock on mine. "The question is, do you love her enough to let her go?"

THIRTEEN

After waking from a nap and taking a shower, I leave the room to find Grim.

"Morning!" Sandy says in the kitchen. "Grumpy pants is waiting for you outside." He points to the backdoor.

I open it to find Grim bent over his motorcycle.

The bike is all chrome and metal muscle, covered in shiny black skin. I step up to the machine and notice the subtle black roses painted around the gas tank. "It's beautiful," I say, placing my palm on the soft worn leather seat.

"Beautiful," Grim agrees, but when I glance up, it's not the bike he's looking at. It's me.

I feel a blush creep onto my cheeks.

"Ever rode on one before?"

"No," I answer, excitement jitters in my stomach.

"Then, let's go," he says.

"Where's Callum?" I ask.

"Nearby. We'll talk about that later. Ride first," he says.

Grim pulls a helmet from under the seat and places it over my head. His cool breath skates over my forehead as he adjusts on the strap under my chin. My skin breaks out in goosebumps, and my heart flutters against my rib cage. Much to my surprise, he straddles the seat and lifts me so I'm sitting in front of him, my legs spread wide on the soft leather.

"Aren't I supposed to sit on the back?"

"You're not used to it yet. It's safer if I surround your body with mine."

My stomach flutters from both his words and his proximity. He revs the engine, and then, we're off.

Riding on a motorcycle is nothing like I've imagined. The power between your legs. No walls to restrict you. No windows to temper your view of the outside world. It's something unlike I've ever experienced before.

It's freedom.

Grim follows a dirt road past the hospital and the field where we found out Mr. Fuzzy met his end. I feel sad for my little, furry friend.

We come to a stop. Grim leaves the engine running.

"Don't take your helmet off. I just want to show you something really quick."

He lifts me off the bike and takes my hand, dragging me to the edge of the woods where what looks like a miniature log cabin was built just a few feet wide in all directions. At the top of the little house are two sticks marked with an X. Carved into the wood was a name. Mr. Fuzzy.

"You did this?" I ask, covering my mouth with my hand in disbelief.

Grim lays a hand on the roof of the little house. "No, Chief David did. He insisted that anything that perishes in this land must return to it. They even gave him a ceremony and laid his feet to the east just as they do their tribe members."

"That's the kindest thing I've ever heard." I lay my hand on the house next to Grim's. He covers my pinky with his.

I close my eyes and whisper, "Sleep well, my friend."

We get back on Grim's bike and travel a few more miles down the road. I look to the clear sky and enjoy the warmth of the sun and the warmth of Grim's skin against my back.

We stop at the edge of a wooded area. Again, he lifts me off and takes my hand guiding toward an overgrown footpath between two large pine trees.

"Look," I say, pointing to the sky.

Grim stops and looks up to the white lines in the sky. "That's what's left behind by airplanes."

I nod. "Whenever I would feel alone, I'd look to the sky and search for airplane trails. It was a reminder that I wasn't alone in the world. There are other people out there, some with even more troubles than my own, some passing right over my head every single day."

"What do you do when you feel alone now?" he asks. I lower my eyes to find him staring at me. "Do you still look to the sky?"

"No," I reply. "I look to you."

Grim's lips turn up at the corners. "You're always surprising me."

I give him a coy, one shoulder shrug. "I'm nothing, if not unpredictable."

"That you are not," he says, tugging me onto the path.

We stop at an overgrown wall. I hear murmurs coming from the other side. I hesitate, digging my shoes into the dirt. "Do you hear that?" I ask.

"Those are our guys. They are lining the entire perimeter of the reservation. ID's are being checked to enter, and the area around the casino is manned to make sure no one leaves there to go elsewhere. All our guys. It's safe. I promise you. This time, it really is safe."

I swallow down my fears.

Grim leans down and takes his knife from his pant

leg. He cuts away at the growth over the wall. Beneath is concrete covered in the usual graffiti. But as he hacks away, I wonder what it is he wants to show me until something else is revealed underneath. It's a painting. Not the usual gang sign or mural to a fallen soldier. An honest to goodness beautiful painting of a girl wearing an oversized t-shirt. Her head is cocked to the side, and she's got a smug expression on her little face. I gasp.

She's holding a kitten. Not just any kitten.

Mr. Fuzzy.

He hacks away at the last of the overgrowth, revealing crazy, blonde curls on the young girl's head.

"It's me," I say in wonder.

"It's you," Grim confirms, stepping back to gauge my expression.

It's not just a caricature of me. It's me. An honest to goodness portrait of what I looked like the day we met. The clothes, the curls, the hair on Mr. Fuzzy, and my little con artist expression. My big, bold eyes. It's more than art.

"It's magic." I press my hand to the wall, stroking it over the insane details. I swing back around to Grim who's still watching me closely, one hand over his chest, the other propping up his chin. "You painted this?"

His answer is a curt nod.

"Grim, you're a painter. A ridiculously talented one."

He shrugs off the compliment, but he can't fool me. I see the way his eyes light up with my words.

"I wanted you to see this because…" He puffs out his cheeks, then exhales in frustration and not being able to find the right words. "Because I *am* the man in the leather hood with bloodied hands, but I'm also more. More than just the reaper of Bedlam. More than just their leader. I'm a man. Flesh and bone. Beating heart. Capable of both life and death. Hate and love. I take, but this…this is my way of…"

"Giving life," I offer.

"Yeah, something like that. I just wanted you to see me. All of me."

I take his face in my hand and stand on my tip-toes. "You think I don't know that you're more?" I slap him lightly on the chest. He grabs my wrist in his hand, and a bolt of awareness sears my skin. "I've known that. I've *always* known that." He releases my wrist. I trail fingertips down his defined chest. I lean in and plant a soft lingering kiss over his heart. "I love you, Grim. All of you. I lift his hand and kiss each of his fingertips. He's watching me closely, following my every move, still as stone. I plant a final kiss on the center of his palm. "Bloodied hands. Beating heart. All of it."

"Fuck, Tricks," he hisses and pulls me up by my arms. We're so close we're breathing each other's air. "It beats for you." His lips descend to mine.

He pulls back. His face looks pained. "Tricks." He rests his forehead on mine. "There's something we need to talk about."

"So, talk," I whisper against his lips.

"Egan is right. It won't be safe for you here."

I still in his arms. "You're pushing me away again."

"I'm not. But you deserve everything this world has to offer. To learn things. To travel. To experience life. To have fucking fun. Things I can't give you. Not now, anyway."

"We don't know that Callum is my father yet —"

"He is. The chief called this morning. It's a ninety-nine-point nine percent match."

I'm not shocked. I knew in my heart he was my father, but hearing the words changes everything. I realize now that Grim knows Callum is my father he will be that much more set on me leaving. "Besides, fun is a foreign concept," I say.

Grim's eyes grow sad, and I realize I've said the wrong thing. "That's just it," he says. "It shouldn't be. Not for you."

"Don't feel sorry for me."

"I'm not feeling sorry for you. But I need you safe. Don't you want to meet your mother? Find out more about your family?"

I'm curious about her, and honestly, I have been thinking about her. What she would sound like. Her mannerisms. If she was kind of funny. If she told the same stories over and over. What kind of music she likes. "Yes. No." I shake my head. "I don't know."

"I talked to her. Your mother."

"You what?" I ask, taken aback.

"Video chat on Callum's phone." He pauses, thinking of his words. "You'll like her. There's nothing not to like about her. She's you. Just older."

I don't know what to say. I do want to meet her. There's no denying it.

"You should go," Grim says. "I can't be looking over my shoulder, wondering if you're okay while I end this war. And you need to find out who you really are."

He's right. I don't want to admit it, but Grim is right. I'm not Emma Jean Parish anymore, but I don't know who Imogen Egan is either. I'm caught between two worlds. I don't know my place in either of them.

"I can't go." I tell him, my eyes welling up with unshed tears. "I won't leave you."

"You can go. You have to go. If I had a chance to see my mother again, I wouldn't hesitate. Go. Live. Experience the world. Meet your family." Grim searches my eyes, and I realize he's not pushing me away. He's pushing me toward something.

I pull him closer. "You're my family."

"I am. Always will be. Distance won't change that. And when it's safe, you can choose to come back."

He's saying the words like he's giving me a choice when I know in the end, he's already made up his mind.

"I will come back," I assure him. "When it's safe, I'll come back."

"Tricks, you don't have to. Don't think of this as a trip with an expiration date. Come back when you truly want to come back, but if you're happy there." He looks into my eyes. "Then, I want you to stay."

"Why...why would you say that?"

"Because this isn't the place for you. Because you deserve more than having to worry about your life. More than what I can give you. Go. Live for fuck's sake. If not for you, then for me. I won't be able to live with myself, knowing you're settling for something when you don't know what else is waiting for you out there."

I choke down a sob. "I'm going to come back," I argue.

My heart is breaking.

I look up at Grim's watery eyes and realize mine isn't the only one.

FOURTEEN

GRIM BREAKS OUR KISS AND SHRUGS OFF HIS JACKET, spreading it open on the grass. He lifts me off my feet, my legs wrapping around his waist as he kneels, setting me down on my back. He resumes his kisses. My lips. My jaw. My neck. I'm writhing underneath of him as he makes his way down my body. His hand slides up my shirt, cupping my breasts as he kneels between my spread legs. My cut-offs are short; with my legs splayed before him every inch of my inner thighs are exposed to him.

Suddenly, Grim's weight is gone, and so are his lips.

I lift my head and am met with dark angry eyes staring between my legs. I clap them shut.

"What the fuck!" he roars. "Tricks, why didn't you

tell me?" A warning rips from deep within his throat. "I'm gonna gut the fucking bastard from groin to heart."

"It wasn't just him," I blurt, needing for him to know the truth. As ugly as it was. "He...he let his men..." I close my eyes tight, unable to say the words. To give new life to a nightmare I don't want to relive.

Grim tips my chin up. "Look at me," he demands.

I comply and am met with the eyes of the devil himself, as dark as the night surrounding us. His stare is as determined as his words. "Then, I'll gut them all."

I've always known that Grim a dangerous man, but I've never felt it in my bones before now. He's all brutality and loyalty. A murderer and a lifesaver. My heart thumps out a warning in my chest that my brain doesn't receive because all I'm thinking is how much I love this man. How much I need him. Not despite who he really is but because of who he is. The bruised and battered place between my thighs pulses and aches. He's so close I can feel his heat on my skin, but not close enough.

"I was going to tell you," I say. "I don't want to keep things from you. But I don't want this to change things between us, either. I don't want your pity or your sympathy."

Grim's chest heaves above me. His nostrils flare. "We can't do this," he says. Burning me with his words.

I try and roll out from under him, but he holds me in place, caging me in with his body.

I push on his chest. "If you don't want me, then why keep me here?"

Grim's brow crinkles with confusion. "No, Tricks. Not because I don't want you. Never that. I want to fuck you more than you could ever understand. More than I can even understand. I just don't want to hurt you."

"Oh," I say.

Grim's expression softens. "Let me make you feel good. Let me erase some of the hurt." He pulls me against him for a searing kiss that makes me want nothing more than for him to be inside of me. Injuries be damned.

His lips release mine all too quickly. The gentle night breeze licks across my wet mouth, cooling my lips.

Grim continues to my neck, sucking behind my ear.

I dig my fingernails into his back as he trails his talented tongue down my shoulder then across my chest. He pushes up my shirt, staring hungrily at my naked breasts. "Perfect, beautiful tits," he whispers with such awe it sounds like a prayer. Sucking my nipple into his warm mouth, he toys with it between his teeth and tongue.

I kick out my legs, needing more. So much more.

"Shhhh...I got you, Tricks."

I groan into the night as he moves to worship my

other nipple. I'm ecstatic and frustrated all at the same time.

He lowers his mouth down my body, trailing his lips across my skin, down past my navel. When he reaches my shorts, he tugs at the button. I lift my hips, to assist him in ridding the barrier of clothing between us.

"Tell me if I hurt you," he murmurs. His breath creates a tingling sensation against my already sensitive and swollen clit.

I can only nod my response because his lips are on me again, silencing my words and consuming my thoughts. He's kissing me passionately in my most intimate place, parting my pussy lips with his tongue and lapping me up like I'm the most delicious morsel he's ever tasted. He groans against my core.

I'm holding onto him, for dear life, my fingers splayed in his hair to anchor him to me and me to the ground.

Grim massages my inner thigh with one hand while he works a thick finger inside of me with the other. Gently, too gently. There is no pain, only Grim and pleasure and everything I want in the world right here between my legs. I tense as he sucks my clit into his mouth. A feeling of pure electric heat sizzles throughout my body. My insides ache as the pressure builds and builds from a spark to a raging fire.

He lifts away slightly, teasing me by blowing softly across my wet pink folds. I shudder so hard my teeth chatter. Arching my back, I pull on his hair, greedily and shamelessly grinding myself against his perfect face. He must like my reaction, because he groans against me, fucking me with his fingers and licking me over and over again like a crazed animal. As if making me come is all that's important in this world.

"I'm close," I tell him, pulling his hair even harder, egging him on.

He lets out a guttural groan, flattening his tongue against my clit, stroking it up and down and back again.

The tension I feel within me is borderline pain, twisting me from the inside out. I'm about to burst through my own skin.

Grim uses his teeth and lightly bites my clit before sucking it hard into his mouth one last time.

I come apart on a roar of my own, screaming his name into the night. I contract around his tongue, coating it in a flush of wetness I can feel dripping down my ass cheeks. The pleasure smashes into me over and over again, shattering me into pieces like a hammer against glass.

For the very first time in my life, I'm happy to be broken.

Grim doesn't allow me to reciprocate. Instead, he dresses me silently and helps me back to the bike. I think he's angry or upset, so I allow him his silence.

When we're back in the room of the brothel, he closes the door and turns the lock.

I remove all of my clothes until I'm standing naked in front of the bed. When he turns from the door, his eyes land on me. His lips part as he takes in my naked form.

I raise my arms out to the side. "I'm bruised and broken. I'm battered and battle-worn. This is who I am. You won't hurt me. I want you to take me. Just as I am." A tear rolls down my cheek.

A growl tears from his throat. He pounces, pushing me back onto the bed. I help him pull off his jacket. He makes quick work of his pants until we're skin on skin. His lips are everywhere. The heat of his thick cock is against my stomach, throbbing against me with need. Moisture leaking from the tip spreads against my skin, and I moan because it's all for me. His need. His love.

I reach down and grab him in my hand, stroking up and down, watching his eyes open and close, his chin tipped up. Knowing I have this much power over such a powerful man makes me drunk with pleasure. I tighten my grip, and he bucks in my hand.

"Enough," he growls, pulling from my grip.

He spreads my legs wide with his knees, and then, he's inside me, filling me, stretching me wide open. Our eyes lock as he begins to fuck me, and I realize he's trying to be gentle.

"You won't hurt me," I whisper, running my hands through his hair. "Please, Grim. I need you. All of you."

That's all it takes. He drives in, thrusting hard, pushing me up further against the headboard. He's relentless as he pounds into me. Pleasure erupts within me, and my stomach tightens with a need for release. He reaches under me and flips me over. He re-enters me with brutal force, lifting my hips to meet his every brutal thrust. It's still not enough. I push back against him. I'm screaming his name, and he's screaming mine until it's all a blur of white light behind my eyes and a full body orgasm that shakes me to my very core, soaking the sheets beneath us.

As I regain my senses, Grim pushes deep inside of me, my name and a swear tears from his throat as he floods me with his release. "Fuck, Tricks!"

We both collapse to the mattress. He flips me back over and settles himself between my thighs. He pushes my hair from my face. "I love you," he says softly. Tears prick my eyes.

"I love you, too."

He buries his face in the nape of my neck, breathing me in. His cock springs to life once more, hardening against my skin. He rolls me to my back, settling between my legs and pushes inside. This time when he begins to rock his hips, it's not a wild animalistic need. It's torturously slow, and passionate.

He lifts his head and stares into my eyes as he makes love to me. Slowly, tenderly, as if for the last time. This goes on for hours, neither one is us wanting it to end. As if my body can't take anymore, I come without warning, violently erupting in a shudder of pleasure. I'm both screaming his name and sobbing as he finds his own release.

When he collapses next to me, I search his face and find that his cheeks are wet. At first, I think it's my own tears smeared across his skin, but then he blinks and a tear of his own pools at the corner of his eye, dropping onto the pillow.

He reaches for a jacket. At first, I think he's already getting dressed, but he pulls something from the pocket and sets the jacket back aside. He lays down beside me once again and lays the cool metal object over my chest and throat.

"My locket," I breathe, clasping a hand over it. Grim places one hand over mine, and the other cups my cheek.

"Why do I feel like this is goodbye?" I whisper, feeling like the breath is being stolen from my lungs little by little. My hearts slows to crawl as if it's pausing to hear what comes next.

Grim's sad golden eyes meet mine. "Because it is."

FIFTEEN

"EJ!" GABBY SAYS WITH AN ENTHUSIASTIC SMILE. She's standing, holding the back of her hospital gown together, one arm tucked behind her back, the other is wrapped in a thick black sling. Sandy is standing on the other side of the bed with a pile of clothes in his arms. He drops it on the bed with a heavy sigh.

"What's wrong?" I ask him.

He looks to Gabby. "You're about to find out."

"Don't mind him. He's just being pouty," Gabby says, sticking her tongue out at Sandy who scrunches his nose in return. I love this playful side of Gabby. A side of her I haven't seen since we were kids.

It's not her playfulness that throws me. It's the familiarity between her and Sandy. I wonder just *how* familiar they've really become.

"Did you hear? I'm being released!" Gabby exclaims.

"Yay," Sandy mutters under his breath.

"No, I haven't heard. That's amazing." I sit on the corner of the bed while she gets dressed. She spins her finger in the air. Sandy rolls his eyes and reluctantly turns around.

"Listen, I have to tell you something," I say. "Actually, I have to ask you something."

"About Ireland?" She jumps up and down then winces, grabbing onto her shoulder.

"You know?"

She pulls a black sundress over her head. Sandy turns back around as if he instinctively knows she's done dressing. I spot a mirror on the wall Sandy was just facing and realize instincts had nothing to do with it. When he spots me looking at the mirror, he flashes me a wink and a sly smile.

"Yes, I know. Callum came in. He told me all about it. Can you believe we're going to Ireland? He says he lives in a town will rolling green hills, and they have festivals and schools. Can you believe it, EJ? We could go to school!"

In all the years I've known Gabby, I've never seen her so excited before.

"And you have a family! A mom and a dad! I can't wrap my brain around this. It's all so...*everything*. It's what we dreamed of, Emma Jean. The day has come when it's all finally coming true. We're getting out of this town. We're going to stop surviving and start actually living."

If I was undecided about leaving before stepping into Gabby's hospital room, I'm not anymore. I can't deny Gabby her safety, this opportunity, or anything that makes her as excited as she is right now.

"We are going to be living our dreams," she repeats, embracing me in a hug.

I stare over her shoulder at a somber-looking Sandy and hold her tightly. "Yeah, we are, Gabby. We finally are."

My words aren't entirely true. They would be if I were speaking them months ago. Over the past few months, my dreams for Gabby have remained the same, but my own have changed. They no longer only include safety and security or a life outside of Lacking.

I dream of a man in a black leather hood, bleeding black roses, and an unbroken heart.

"THAT'S A DIRTY TRICK YOU PULLED," I say, crossing my arms over my chest.

Callum is sitting at the table, typing away at a laptop. When he sees me, he closes it and removes the reading glasses from his nose, tucking them into his coat pocket.

"I supposed you've spoken to Gabriella, then," he says with an unapologetic smile. "I didn't get to where I am by playing by the rules, and neither did your beau for that matter."

I stand in front of him across the table.

"Sit," he says, holding his hand out to a chair.

"I'd rather stand." I say, steeling my nerve. "You want me to come to Ireland with you, right?"

"Aye, you and Gabriella."

"Then, I have demands."

"Demands?" he asks with a sparkle in his eye.

"Yes, you're a businessman. You didn't get to where you are now without negotiating a time or two."

"Is that what this is then? A negotiation?"

"Yes."

"Did Grim send you? I expected him to make some demands of me in exchange for allowing you to come with me, but he hasn't. The only thing he asked is that if you were to come that your friend Gabriella come as well. Are you here as his ambassador?"

"No. Grim didn't make any demands of you because he loves me. He's not going to negotiate the terms of my release because I'm not his possession. These are my own."

He nods and looks pleased. "Sit then. Business conducted standing tells the other person you don't trust them."

"I don't trust you."

"Yes, but you have to give an air of trust to make the other person want to give in to your demands. Without trust, negotiations seldom get far." He leans back in his chair.

I round the table and take the seat opposite him. I fold my hands on the table. "Better?" I raise my eyebrows.

"Much. So, go on then, what are these demands of yours? Shall I make a list?" He picks up a pen from the table and pulls a small note pad from his pocket.

I shake my head. "No, I don't need this to be written down. You never know who might see it."

He smiles proudly. "Smart girl." He places the pen and pad down next to his laptop. He gestures to me, then crosses his legs. "Go ahead."

I clear my throat. "Do you, I mean, does Clan Egan run girls?"

"Aye," he answers, without hesitation. "We don't traffic if that's what you're asking. Your mother would have my bloody head, but we run some establishments up and down the East coast and several back in Ireland."

"Good. You see, because of the violence here in Lacking and the war breaking out. Girls, I mean women, are scared to come here and work for Bedlam, regardless of the promised increase in security measures and the chief opening the back road through the reservation so the guests and staff don't have to drive through Los Muertos territory to get here. Most of the girls who had signed on to start during the grand opening have quit and won't agree to come back until it's safe."

"I've heard this. What exactly is it you're asking of me, Imogen?"

I lean my elbows on the table and hold his curious gaze. I straighten my spine. "I'm asking that you send girls to the brothel. Temporarily, of course, until the war is over and those positions can be given to the willing women of Lacking who desperately need employment."

"Done," he says. "Anything else?"

"I want you to send men to help Grim and Bedlam fight the war."

"Already done. It's my war to fight, too. Just because I won't be present for it doesn't mean the clan won't be. I've told Grim as much."

I nod.

"I want you to stop dealing heroin here."

"It's not as if I'm going to continue business with Marco, or whoever his predecessor might be. I've already reached out to Margaret. Los Muertos won't be involved in any of my business dealings in Lacking."

"No, you don't understand. I want you to stop dealing heroin in Lacking. For good."

Callum raises his eyebrows. "And why should I do that?"

"Because I won't go with you if you don't. The people of this town suffer from poverty. Poverty leads them to desperation and a need for an escape. That escape comes in the form of pain pills, which get them hooked on heroin because it's cheaper and has a stronger effect. Addiction leads to crimes against innocent people and senseless violence. The gang violence is one thing; the violence among the people is another. If I can help stop it, I will. And it starts with you."

Callum considers me for a moment. "Is that negotiable?"

I shake my head. "I won't come with you if you don't stop dealing in this town."

"If I don't, someone else will. The cartel has a presence here."

"Then, I also amend my request that you deal with them as well, on whatever terms that won't turn them against you or cause more violence."

Callum leans forward, mimicking my position. "Done. Anything else?"

"One more thing," I sing softly.

"Go on." Callum says, intrigued.

"The second I want to come back, you'll let me."

"Imogen. I'm not your captor. You're my daughter. If and when you want to come back, I'll have the plane fueled up and on the runway within the hour."

"Good. Then, it's a deal."

"I amend that to say, when it's safe. I won't bend where your safety is concerned. It's non-negotiable."

"Agreed," I hold out my hand. Callum takes it in his, and we shake. He stands from the table, still holding my hand, and pulls me from my seat into an embrace. He smells like springtime aftershave and cigar smoke. It feels new to be embracing my father, but not entirely uncomfortable. I relax in his arms.

"We seem to have reached a deal," he says, resting his chin on my head. "Which is a good thing because your mother would've had my balls on a pike in the driveway the second I landed and you weren't on the plane."

I pull away. "She sounds...menacing."

"More like formidable. Much like yourself. People may think I'm the one they should fear, but they've never crossed the likes of your mother."

SIXTEEN

I KNOW THE INSTANT I ENTER THE ROOM THAT TRICKS is already gone. I both hate and am grateful for her wanting to skip the hard goodbyes. On the middle of the bed is a quote scribbled on a napkin.

> *How lucky I am to have something that makes saying goodbye so hard."*

— WINNIE THE POOH.

Instead of a signature, there's a doodle of a simple black rose at the bottom.

I hold the note to my chest and close my eyes. Trying to steady the erratic heartbeat that feels a lot like I'm being stabbed with each breath.

"Boss? There's a bus full of Irish women out front."

"What?" I spin to face Sandy.

"Why?"

"They said they're here to work at the brothel. I believe they called themselves *temps*."

"Who would—" I pause. "Irish?" I ask.

Sandy nods. "Every last one of them. I figured you asked Callum to send them. Negotiated terms for Gabby and EJ going…"

"The only thing I asked for was that he keep them safe."

"Well, then this is either from the kindness of Callum's heart or…"

I smile, knowing full well who was responsible. "It's not."

Alby appears in the hall. "You're right. It's not from the goodness of his heart, and yes, there was a negotiation."

"I still don't get it," Sandy whines.

"Tricks. She negotiated terms with Callum."

"She sent you a bus load of Irish whores?" Sandy asks. "A bit of an odd choice for a going away present."

"Aye, she did," Alby says with a laugh. "If she were anyone else, we'd be in for a fight, but Callum's so proud he'd send over every woman in Ireland if it pleased her."

"What else did she negotiate?" I ask, curiously.

"We stop dealing heroin in Lacking, and that we send

you men to fight your war. They're waiting for you, with your own men, in your war room."

"When did this all take place?"

"A few hours before they got on the plane. Why?"

I shake my head. "No reason."

Alby tips his hat. "I'll be off now. Got a family of my own to see to back home." He leaves, whistling the same damn catchy tune that's been playing in my head for the past several days.

"What was that all about? Why it is important when she negotiated with Callum?" Sandy whispers in case Alby is still in hearing distance.

"Because Tricks had already decided to go before she talked to Callum."

Sandy smiles. "It wasn't a negotiation at all."

I chuckle and shake my head. "It was a con."

Sandy chuckles then stops and snaps his fingers. "Oh, what Alby just said. His men are in the war room with ours. That's what I was coming to tell you."

You ready for this?" Haze asks, from where he's just appeared behind Sandy, leaning against the doorframe.

Without having to worry over Trick's safety, I can dive into the deepest, darkest place in my soul and be the monster I need to be, the one who's been waiting to see Marco die for far too long.

So, it begins, I think to myself.

I pocket Tricks's quote. "I'm ready," I rasp.

"Good. Rollo is going to take Mona to his cabin until we make a decision on what to do with her," Haze says as I lead the way to the back door.

As much as I want to give the go ahead to send Mona across the river in the reapers boat, it's not my decision to make, it's up to Tricks, but she's not here. Mona will just have to ride out her time with Rollo until she gets back.

If she gets back, an annoying voice in my head reminds me.

I stop in my tracks as an idea strikes. "Tell Rollo to be ready when we call, I think I know of a way we can use Mona if it comes down to it."

"How?" Sandy asks.

The time for goodbyes is over. The time for war is now.

I look to my brothers. "As bait."

SEVENTEEN

WE LAND IN A PRIVATE AIRFIELD IN IRELAND WHERE A private car is waiting to take us to our final destination. Over an hour later and still trapped in the car, I'm dozing off with my forehead up against the glass when Gabby smacks my arm.

"Look!" she says, pointing out the window. We've just arrived in a village. Cobblestone streets. Perfectly symmetrical stone houses line the square. Each with exactly six windows in the front and a single door directly in the center. Flower boxes under the windows spill over with bright pink and purple.

"You live here?" Gabby asks Callum.

He chuckles. "Yes, and no. This is our village, but we live up the hill, not in town."

"It looks like a fairytale," I whisper, pressing my

fingers and nose against the glass. I'm reminded of another time Gabby and I were brought to a new home. A day I'll never forget because it was one of the worst days of my life. Marco. Los Muertos. It all started on that day. I begin to feel uneasy. My stomach rolls.

After a few minutes of winding roads surrounded by lush green hillside, Gabby hits me once again. "If the village is a fairytale, then this is where the prince must live."

On the top of the hill at the end of a dirt drive is a tall, dark stone structure, complete with castle-like roof top and intricate stone carvings over every window. In front, there's a steep staircase with a fountain at the end of a large square pool/lake in the center of the rounded dirt drive.

"Holy shit," I say, with my mouth agape. "Where are we?"

"We are at Egan Castle," Callum announces as the car stops at the center of the driveway. "Otherwise known as home."

"Holy fucking shit," Gabby whispers, staring up at the five-story castle in wonderment. The brick is a color mix between gray and beige covered sporadically with green moss. "What is that part called?" Gabby asks, pointing to the uneven roofline.

"Ah, that's called a battlement," Callum answers, his face lighting up. "You see where the gaps are? The lower parts? That's where the soldiers or guards would shoot arrows at intruders."

"Did your ancestors live here?" Gabby asks enthusiastically.

Callum snickers. "No, Ireland was one of the first countries to dismantle the aristocracy. No royalty in my blood. The wife and I bought the castle ourselves and gutted the inside to put in new modern...well, everything. When Imogen was taken from us," he pauses, "we always knew we'd get her back one day, and when that day came, we needed the safest home we could get our hands on."

He looks up to find Gabby and I staring at him. He pulls his frown into a smile. "And there isn't anything safer than Egan Castle."

Gabby scrunches her nose. "Where do you even look to buy a castle? Do you call your local castle realtor?"

Callum shrugs. "I suppose you could, but we bought this one online."

She gasps. "A castle website?"

"Nae, Craigslist."

We don't have time to laugh because the front doors fly open. The woman who runs out with her hand over her throat, searching with her eyes through the dark-tinted car windows, could be my clone if not for the dark circles lining her eyes.

My mother.

The nerves I'd been feeling throughout the entire trip slowly begin to dissipate as a sense of comfort and familiarity wash over me with just one glance at the woman who gave birth to me.

This definitely isn't like the last time we were brought to a new home.

It's been going on eighteen years now since I've seen her last. I can't wait another minute more. I fling open the car door and race toward her. She sees me and breaks out in a full sprint, flying down the steps. At the bottom of those steps, we crash into each other's arms with a violent smack of an embrace.

We stand there sobbing, holding on for dear life. We're strangers, but we're not. This person loves me unconditionally. I feel it in my bones, in my hair. I've been skeptical of every person I've ever laid eyes on, and considering my past, I know it's foolish to jump into the river...er mote, without a life raft, but this is my mother. My *mother*.

"Hi, *mom*?" I whisper into her neck.

She smiles into my hair.

Gabby clears her throat from behind us. We both look up to where she's standing beside the car with Callum, a reluctant look on her tanned face.

My mother sniffles and releases one arm from me, holding it open to Gabby. Gabby drops her backpack to the dirt and runs into our hug.

The three of us soak each other's clothes with our tears. I don't know who stumbled first, but rather than let go, we fall to a crumpled heap right there on the driveaway.

Callum comes over to help his half-crying, half-laughing wife off the driveway. He wraps his arm around her and smiles proudly down at us. His own eyes are both weary from the travel and filled with emotion.

My mother looks from me and Gabby like she can't believe we're really here. She speaks for the first time, and hearing her voice is like a song from the past, filled with nothing but pure joy. "Welcome home, my girls."

THE INSIDE of the castle looks nothing like the outside. It's not dark or musty. It's open and airy. Clean and modern with a white and grey color pallet and stainless-steel fixtures.

My mother shows Gabby and I to our rooms. They are across the hall from one another on the fifth floor. Each one is clean yet plush and luxurious. Flat screen TVs mounted to the walls above the dressers. A laptop on a well-appointed desk for each of us.

The closets have several pairs of jeans and t-shirts in different sizes. All new with tags. "I didn't know what size you were, so I figured I'd just get the basics and the three of us could go shopping for a full wardrobe."

From across the hall, Gabby squeals with delight.

"What was that?" My mother asks.

"That was Gabby, opening the closet."

She laughs and watches me as I take in the well-appointed bathroom. "There's everything you need as far as toiletries go. Again, I didn't know what you liked, so I didn't get any makeup or things of the sort. We'll add it to our list when we go into town."

I sit on the edge of the bed. "You don't have to do all this for us. We've never had anything like... it's too much."

My mother sits next to me and puts her arms around me. "Nonsense. Think of it like this. I've missed years of spoiling you. I'm going to make up for lost time. Will you please indulge your ma and allow me to spoil her daughter?"

"And there's a tub in the bathroom!" Gabby's shout echoes into the room.

"Daughters," she corrects herself with a happy sigh.

"Thank you," I say, giving in.

"What else might you want to do? What are your interests?"

I frown. "Do you want to hear the truth, or would you rather I come up with a less unsettling lie?" I ask.

"The truth, my dear."

I inhale deeply. "I'm a con artist. A master liar. I can pick pockets with the best of them and make people believe obvious lies. I passed a lie detector test once with the sheer force of my talent."

My mother frowns.

"I should have gone with the lie."

Her lips twitch, a dimple forcing its way to the surface of her cheek, and I realize she's holding back laughter. And failing.

"What?" I ask.

"Oh, wait until I tell Callum." She slaps her leg.

"What's so funny?"

She clears her throat and lays a reassuring hand on my shoulder. "When Callum and I met, he was working as a guard at the local jail and me? Well, I was the first inmate to ever give him trouble."

"You were an inmate?"

"It was a local jail. Just an overnight jaunt."

"What were you there for?" I ask, already knowing the answer when my mother's smile turns into a full-face beam of bright white teeth.

"Pick pocketing."

This time I join her in her laughter, and when Gabby comes in to ask what's going on, we recover just enough to tell her before starting all over again.

I CAN'T SLEEP. It's after midnight, and I've tossed and turned. The bed is the most comfortable I'd ever been in, but it's my restless mind not my level of comfort that keeps me awake.

Finally, after trying for hours, I get up. I'm not thirsty or hungry or in search of anything. I find myself wondering the halls of the massive castle, shuffling my feet against the plush carpet. I see a light on in the living room. I peek around the corner and there's my mother, staring off into the fire. I step into the room, and she looks up at me with tear-filled eyes.

"What's wrong?" I ask, crouching before her.

She wipes at her eyes as she shakes her head, her curls sway softly against her face. She closes her robe tighter. "Nothin' I'm just...I'm so happy your home I'm afraid if I go to sleep I'll wake to discover it all just a lovely dream."

"I'm here. I'm real," I assure her taking her hand.

She pulls me down onto the sofa next to her.

"Now, why don't you tell me all about this beau of yours."

"I've never met him but for the one video call. I'm familiar with Belly and Marci, though, and never heard a bad word spoken about the man."

"I didn't know him long, but Belly was great. Grim loved him very much." I hesitate, unsure exactly of what to say about Grim. About what we have. About where we stand now.

We sit in silence for a few moments, staring at the fire. "Do you know what Imogen means?" she asks, breaking the silence.

I shake my head.

"It means 'last born daughter'. Because you were a miracle, and we knew there would be no more coming after you." She sighs. "I downright hated your father for so long after you were taken from us. But he grew up in this life, and I knew what I was getting into when I married him, so it was as much my fault as it was his."

"No, you can't blame yourself for things that happen to you."

She gives me a squeeze. "And neither can you."

She has a point.

My mother nudges my side. "Go on then. Tell me all about your beau."

Having experienced a lifetime of little comfort, I find it odd now to be as at ease with her as I am in my own skin. I take a deep breath and tell her all about Grim. How we met as kids. How we had an instant connection. How we were apart for years but had never forgotten about one another. I don't even realize I'm crying until she wraps her arm around me and pulls me in, tucking me into her body.

"There there, now. No need for tears darling. You'll see your beau again. I know it."

"How can you be so sure?" I sniffle.

"Because true love cannot be separated by time or space." She tips my chin up, and I find myself looking into an almost identical pair of eyes. "Do you truly love this boy?"

I answer honestly. "With all that I am."

"Then, you'll find a way back to one another," she says, like it's a fact.

"How can you be so sure?"

"Because," she smiles. "You're here now, aren't you?"

My heart warms.

She lifts the blanket over my shoulders. "And because I'm your mother. You'll learn soon enough that mothers know everything, and we are always right."

I relax against my mother, and after a few moments of comfortable silence, we both fall peacefully asleep.

EIGHTEEN

Levi Cohen, along with his wife Leigh, own the only deli in Lacking. It doesn't have a name, or at least, I don't think it does. The sign above the barred door simply reads DELI. Belly, my brothers, and I used to take up residence at one of only two tables inside most Sunday afternoons. We'd stuff our faces with Levi's famous pastrami sandwiches while Belly and Levi laughed or argued about football or something that happened during their weekly poker game.

Although the deli is positioned between Immortal Kings and Bedlam Territory, Levi and Leigh aren't affiliated with any particular organization. However, they're friends, not just of Bedlam, but to my family. Which is why Sandy and I are here now, taking in the aftermath of this morning's drive-by.

"Holy shit," I mutter, crouching low in the passenger seat, pulling my hood further over my face. "It's worse than I thought."

Sandy grumbles his agreement as he slows the van to a crawl.

The front windows are blown out, glass shards scattered all over the street and sidewalk, twinkling as they reflect the last rays of the fading afternoon sun. The thick metal DELI sign now hangs sideways, swaying back and forth like a dying man calling out one last time for help. Glass crunches underneath the weight of the tires just as the sign drops face-first onto the sidewalk below.

Sandy parks the van in the alley behind the butcher shop and cuts the engine. We look around to make sure we aren't spotted before heading inside the deli using the back entrance through the small prep area.

There's a long trail of smeared red leading behind the counter where Sandy and I find Levi, sitting up with his back against a cabinet, clutching a bottle of whiskey by the neck. His dead wife draped over his lap.

"Fuck, Levi," I start, unsure of what to say next.

Levi's grey and black hair is tousled. His white beard is stained red at the ends. His eyes are glassy and unfocused. He takes a long pull from the bottle, but doesn't look up at us.

"You know," he starts. "There used to be a such a thing called honor amongst thieves. Where innocents weren't subjected to the violence between organizations. I served in the Israeli army for two years, as did my wife. We both saw death on a daily basis, and caused much death ourselves. But that was a fight against an enemy who fought back. It was soldier against soldier. Our bullets never strayed far from their intended targets."

"Fuck," Sandy curses, pulling at his hair and puffing out his cheeks. "Shit is bad, Grim."

At the mention of my name Levi finally looks up. He looks over my shoulder. I turn to see what he's looking at, but no one is there. "I guess you really are the reaper," he says, unblinking. He looks over my shoulder once more.

Still no one.

"What is it?" I ask. Crouching down beside him I pull my hood from my face. "What are you looking for?"

"I'm looking for her," he says, gently smoothing down his wife's hair with a shaky hand.

"She's gone," I remind him.

"Yes, but you're dead. If you're here, then I must dead too. Which means that Leigh is probably looking for me. She'll be cross if she thinks I'm hiding from her. Although, when I find her I have to tell her that I never expected the Grim Reaper to actually be Grim the reaper of Bedlam." He chuckles. "She'll get a kick out of it."

I place my hand on his shoulder. "Levi, you're not dead, and neither am I."

"I'm not?" he asks, his words weighted with the sound of disappointment.

"No, I'm sorry. You're not."

He closes his eyes tightly. "Grim, the innocent shouldn't have to suffer. Not like this."

I agree.

Either Marco doesn't believe me and my brothers are dead, or my plan has backfired and he's pecking at what he thinks are the dying bones of Bedlam in an attempt to take over our business. It's not just Bedlam he wants to destroy. The Kings have been under attack, as well as anyone who's ever been associated with Bedlam, all while Marco remains in hiding while his soldiers slaughter innocents.

"Life can't go on like this," Levi sobs.

"It won't." I assure him, standing up and glancing over the warn torn deli. The table where we used to sit is one of the only things left untouched by a bullet.

Levi's head falls back against the cabinet. "You can't take over a town if there isn't a town left." He looks to his wife again and sobs. "I have nothing left."

And I mean it—it won't go on—even if it I have to show my face to get to Marco.

I look to Sandy who's staring at Leigh's lifeless body with a pained look on his face.

"Sandy," I say. His eyes snap to mine.

He follows me over to the other side of the deli.

"Make some calls. I want a brother of Bedlam posted inside every business in this town whose doors are still open. They'll stay from open 'til close, and offer people rides to and from work."

Sandy pulls his phone from his pocket "On it," he says, tapping away at the screen as he moves to the center of the room.

A loud, popping sound pierces the quiet. A picture on the wall behind Sandy cracks and falls to the ground, followed by a barrage of bullets.

"Shit," Sandy shouts.

I leap over a table and shove him violently, landing on top of him behind a refrigerated case. Bullets pepper the walls until the sound of tires screeching against the pavement outside signal the end.

Sandy grabs his gun and runs to the front door. I race over to the counter on the other side. Before I see Levi, I spot the bottle of whiskey several feet from the counter, broken. What's left of it is spinning in a spilt pool of amber-colored liquid.

I crouch beside him once more. "Levi," I say. He doesn't move.

I pull on his shoulder gently. His head rolls to face me. His eyes are wide open is his mouth. The side of his neck is covered in blood.

Levi is dead.

"Fuck!" I roar, punching my hand through the cabinet door. This war needs to end, and it won't unless we do something more than point and shoot. We need to be cleverer. We need..."

Trick's beautiful face comes to mind.

We need a con.

Sandy is winded as he approaches, tucking his gun away. "The car was too far away by the time I got out there. I blew out the back windshield, but I don't think I hit—" he stops abruptly when he sees Levi and my bleeding knuckles.

I reach out and close Levi's lifeless eyes. "Go," I tell him softly. "Go find her."

FRESH FROM THE hell I've just witnessed, I burst into the chief's office.

He looks up, startled, then relaxes once he realizes it's me. "You're going to give an old man a heart attack if you keep entering my office like you've got a bomb strapped under your jacket."

I stand next to the chief's desk. "After you found out that Emma Jean isn't of tribal blood, what did you do with the application?"

The chief raises his eyebrows. He opens a drawer and

129

digs through to the bottom. "We normally send out a letter of denial, but I figured I'd hang tight on this one, given the circumstances."

I shake my head. "No, send it, but not a denial. An approval."

"Why would I do..." the chief pauses. "Oh, I see. And by chance, do you want me to ask him to come in to receive his first check?"

"He's probably learned by now that I'm dead." I shrug. "If he believes it, then there's no reason for him to think he's not welcome on the reservation."

"He'll wonder why we aren't asking him to bring his wife along," the chief says, turning in his chair.

"Write the letter personally, as Emma Jean's father. Tell him that, as he must know by now, she's disappeared after being taken into custody by Lemming, but in her absence, you want to bless your new son -in -law with all that he's entitled to by tribal law."

He steeples his hands and purses his lips. "I don't know. He knows I've had trouble with his old man. You think he'll buy it?"

"We can't be sure until we try. Tell him you've had a change of heart since learning Emma Jean is your daughter. And the time to make peace is now. Tell him you want Los Muertos to run security. Tell him anything that might feed his fucking ego and get him on the reservation."

"What kind of ritual?" he asks, skeptically.

I lean over the desk. "A deadly one."

NINETEEN

"GABBY, I HATE TO SAY THIS BECAUSE I DON'T WANT the compliment going to your head…" I say, staring at her reflection in the mirror from behind her.

"What?" she asks, setting down the tube of mascara in her hand.

I smile. "You get prettier every day."

She blushes and then shrugs and turns back to the mirror, observing her reflection. For the first time since I can remember, she appears happy to see the person staring back at her. "I feel prettier every day."

"I think that's what it is."

She looks at me through the mirror. Her expression soft. "Thanks, EJ." She wrinkles her nose. "Should I still call you EJ? I just realized that it really doesn't make sense anymore since your name is Imogen and not Emma

Jean." Gabby applies gloss to her lips. Her eyes are heavily lined. Over the past several weeks, I've seen her grow stronger. Bolder. More confident. The evidence is in the makeup she's grown to love and wears every day, even if we aren't going out. I love watching her shine come back after so many years. It makes me so happy. And...nauseous?

I grab my churning stomach. "Oh, shit."

"Again?" Gabby asks, swiveling on her stool.

There's no time to answer. I race for the bathroom and barely make it to the toilet, emptying the contents of my stomach in several loud heaves so violent I wouldn't be surprised if I expelled a vital organ or two into the white porcelain.

When I think it's passed and there's nothing left to puke up, I slowly stand on wobbly legs and flush. I wash my hands and splash some water on my face.

"I don't think Irish food agrees with me," I groan to a sympathetic Gabby as I skulk back into our room.

"You've been working yourself too hard. All those hours with the tutor or in class, and then when you come home, you're in the gym for hours with the trainer. You don't rest enough."

"That might be true," I grumble.

Gabby stands and opens her arms, and I fall into them, jumping back with a shock of pain.

"What now?" she asks.

My hands cover my breasts over my shirt. "Just sore. Probably that time of the month soon."

Gabby eyes me suspiciously, then crosses the room to the dresser. She sits and picks up a hairbrush and begins to casually brush her hair. "So, when would you say the last time you had that time of the month was?"

I fall onto the mattress. "I've never been regular. You know that." I try to recall my last actual period. "But I had something after we got here. Yeah, I did. I think."

"Something like a period?"

"Spotting more like." As the words leave my mouth, dread pools in my stomach.

I sit up. My face pales. I reach out and hold onto one of the bed posts to keep from toppling over.

"Oh, shit." Gabby runs to my side.

"What if..." I whisper. I don't have to finish the sentence. I don't know how. There's too many what-ifs. *What if I really am? What if Grim isn't the father? What if it's one of those men Marco let play with me like a dog toy? Or Marco himself?*

"I think I'm going to be sick again."

Gabby races to the bathroom. She emerges quickly, setting a wastepaper basket on my lap. I hug it for dear life. Rocking back and forth on the edge of the bed.

Gabby sits down beside me and gently rubs my back. "It's going to be okay. We'll get a test and figure this out together."

"But what if—"

"Shhhh. It's too early for what ifs. One thing at a time."

"What on earth is the matter?" My mother asks from the doorway. She's clutching a stack of folded towels, which she immediately drops to the floor. She rushes into the room and kneels before me.

I swallow hard, but can't find the words. I look to Gabby, giving her silent permission.

Gabby gets the message. She clears her throat. "How soon would you say is too soon to come to you with a major life problem?"

Ma looks from Gabby back to me. She places a reassuring hand on my knee. "You're scaring the ever loving' shite out of me, girls. Out with it."

The nausea passes, at least for the moment. I take a deep breath and set the wastepaper basket on the floor. I don't even realize my hands are cradling my stomach until my mother's eyes follow.

She places both her hands over my own and smiles up at me. "That ain't no problem, my dear." She squeezes my hands and shakes her head. "It's a babe."

IT'S LATE AT NIGHT, but I can't sleep. I wander the halls until I find the room I'm looking for, getting lost twice in the twisted halls of the castle. When I'm almost sure I'm in the right place I knock softly on what I hope is the door to Callum's study.

"Come in," he answers.

I push open the heavy oak door. The castle had been updated to look modern and bright, except this room. It was dark and covered with heavy furnishings. The walls were a dark oak matching the formattable desk. Which is where I expect to find him, but when his chair is empty I glance around.

"Over here," he says. He's on the other side of the room, sitting in a high-backed chair with a drink in hand, staring off into the fireplace.

He glances up at me and offers me a small smile. "Come, sit with me."

I take the chair opposite him. Regardless of the roaring fireplace, a chill runs down my arms and legs. I rub up and down the arms of my thick hoodie.

"Here," Callum says, pulling a heavy wool blanket from the back of his own chair. Leaning over, he sets it across my lap. "Better?"

I hold the blanket closed in the front and relax a little into the warmth. Between that and the fireplace, I'm almost comfortable. Almost. "Much better. Thank you. The weather here is a little different than Florida."

"It takes some getting used to," Callum replies, taking a sip from his drink. He crosses his leg over his opposite knee and resumes staring at the fireplace. A few moments of silence pass between us.

"Listen," I start. "Are you…" I struggle with finding the right word. "Disappointed in me?"

Callum regards me for a beat. "Nae, I'm not disappointed in you. Am I still gonna give Grim a beating on for knocking up my little girl?" He nods as if he's agreeing with himself. "Most certainly. But you—" His expression softens. "I'll be happy as long as you are happy."

His words do more to warm me than the blanket.

"Happy?" I ask with a burst of a laugh. I look to my hands. If only it were that easy. If only it were Grim's baby growing inside of me.

"What's the matter?" Callum asks, his brows wrinkled with concern.

I tug the blanket around me tighter.

"I told Ma what happened to me while I was at Los Muertos. I don't know if you know…" I trail of. It's too hard. I'm not going to be able to tell him.

"Aye, I know, but don't be cross with your ma. She didn't tell me. Grim did. A ways back." He cocks his head to the side. "You know, I'm a daft man at times. I realize now what that look of worry is, and I think my own excitement of having you here has caused me to overlook somethings I'd rather not think about."

"I know the feeling."

"So, your look of worry is because you don't know if Grim is the father." He doesn't pose it as a question.

I press my hand over my stomach inside the blanket as tears prick my eyes. "I don't know if it's him," I admit. "And chances are, after what...chances are it's not."

"I'm sorry," he offers.

"Don't be."

"Not for what you've been through. You don't need me to be sorry for you. I know that much about you. I'm sorry for being a shite father." He sighs.

I'm about to argue with him when he holds up his hand to prevent me. "You and Gabby are both going to see a therapist the soonest I can schedule it. You need to talk to someone. A professional. You've got to work through the past," he says, his eyes dropping to my concealed midsection. "Before you can make a sound decision about your future."

"Thank you," I manage to say. I don't know if a therapist would be helpful, but neither is losing sleep while my thoughts go around in a highway of circles with no off ramp.

"I'd offer for you to see the town priest, but I don't take you for the religious type," he says.

"I'm not, although I'm sure he's very helpful. But I don't think I'd feel comfortable talking about all of those things him. The violence and all, with a man of a god I don't think I believe in."

Callum's laugh surprises me. When he sees me staring, he explains. "You're in Ireland, Imogen. The priests can be the most violent of us all."

TWENTY

It's been months. I'm starting to think Marco isn't going to reply to the chief's request for him to show his face on the reservation, and we've had no luck in finding him. According to sources, he's not in the Los Muertos compound and hasn't been since the day I challenged him to a fight we never got a chance to finish. Yet the violence in Lacking continues to grow with each passing day, which makes me believe Marco couldn't have gone far and that he's still in control of Los Muertos.

"The bastard bought it. He's here!" Sandy exclaims out of breath. "The chief just sent me a text."

I grab my jacket and head for the door. "Where?" I ask.

"On top of the hill, by the far wall."

We run to the van that's already parked in the back. Haze is behind the wheel. The second we close the doors, we take off.

We get to the hill, and I draw my gun as we slowly creep up the side. It's not until we get to the top that I realize there is no need for my weapon.

The chief is standing behind Mal and Marco, who are buried up to their necks in an ant pile, groaning and screaming as they're eaten alive by the tiny insects.

"It can't be you," Marco whispers as realization sets in, followed by disappointing rage. He growls and waves his head violently from side to side but gives up when he realizes there is no escaping the trap he's been buried in. "No! You're dead!"

I smirk. "The Grim Reaper doesn't die. But you do."

Marco mutters something incoherent.

I kneel before him and press my gun to his forehead. "Ants? A bit dramatic, don't you think, Chief?"

"Not dramatic. This is nature's jail," The chief explains. He looks to my hand. "No. No guns."

"What?" I ask, standing up while Marco and Mal turn their heads from side to side, trying their best to flick off the invading ants but only angering them further.

"You cannot shoot someone on these lands. It's tribal law, and I forbid it."

"And you think death by fire ants is a better idea?" I raise an eyebrow.

"It's more creative," the chief mumbles. "But no, your issue is with Marco. Mal will die by fire ants. You will use your hands to take down your enemy as a warrior. There's no glory in guns."

"It's faster," Haze argues.

"Touché," the chief agrees, "but rules are rules, son. Rituals. Holy places. All those things." He widens his stance and crosses his arms, and I know he won't budge. I could just shoot Marco in the head. Ask forgiveness, not permission. But, I can't do that to the chief, and there's something thrilling that makes my mouth water as I think about tearing Marco limb from limb.

Marco spits, "I'll kill you, motherfucker."

I take off my jacket and hand it to Haze. Sandy takes my gun.

I look to the chief, who's smiling.

I open my arms wide. "By all means. Dig the mother-fucker up."

Two of the chief's inner circle work to dig Marco free of the ants. His black eyes never leave mine. He stops flinching as the ants continue their assault on his face.

Once Marco is free from the pile, he slaps the ants from his skin, then wastes no time, roaring at me like a crazed lunatic.

"I should've mentioned," the chief calls out. "The ant

bites promote a surge of adrenaline before they bite enough to actually kill."

I duck, escaping contact with Marco's fist.

Marco isn't fighting me as a man. He's crazed and bloodthirsty. A demon who doesn't care if he goes down, as long as he takes me with him. That makes two of us.

He manages to land a few blows and me several of my own until we're wrestling down the hill. We crash into Sandy, who falls over us. Marco lunges for Sandy, pulling his weapon from his waistband. He swirls it around and aims it at my head. I push my head against the barrel of his gun as victory dances in his eyes. "This is it, Grim. It's over for you."

"Marco! Help!" comes a shout in the distance.

Marco's gaze shifts to where Mona is standing on top of the hill with Rollo by her side. She's not in distress as her yell indicated. In fact, she's the opposite. She looks cool and calm as she raises her hand and gives Marco the middle finger.

The entire episode is only a fraction of a second, but it's all I need. Marco refocuses his attention on me, but he's not quick enough. I lunge forward and knock the gun from his hands. I land on top of him, and I swing my fist with all of my force against his head. I'm not punching him. I'm punching through him. His skull cracks under my knuckles, but I'm still not done. Over and over again, I pummel the fucker. Blood splatters on my face and in my eyes, and I don't care. I throw blow after blow until Marco gurgles through the blood, until the gurgles cease and so does Marco.

Power surges through me as the life force drains from his body. I'm disappointed that it's over so soon, but regardless that he's dead, I'm not done killing him. Not yet. I scream and rage and continue to pummel him, crazed with power and revenge and adrenaline.

"Enough," Sandy says, pulling me off Marco.

I spit on Marco's body. "Now, you really are Los Muertos, motherfucker."

I look up to the chief. "Are the ancestors satisfied?"

"What? Oh, the gun thing?" the chief shrugs and waves his hand dismissively. "That's not really a thing." He pulls a large barreled silver gun with a wooden handle from under his jacket and pumps a single bullet into Mal's skull. "Thank god. His shrieking and wailing was giving me a fucking migraine," the chief says, rubbing his temple with the butt of his weapon.

"Then, why?" I ask, still out of breath, covered in Marco's blood.

The chief smiles. "I didn't want to rob you of the satisfaction of killing him with your bare hands. Feels good, doesn't it?"

Sandy and Haze are both chuckling as I glance down one last time at what's left of Marco. I slowly raise my eyes back to face the chief. "It feels fucking amazing."

"Good, then it worked. You can thank your girl," he says. "She knew it would be better this way."

"Tricks," I say her name on my lips. I ball my fists, waiting for the anger of her interfering to come, but it doesn't. Instead, I throw my head back and run my blood covered fingers through my hair.

And I laugh. I laugh so long and hard my ribs ache and my chest hurts. I drop to my knees in the dirt as the sky opens up and the rain washes Marco's blood from my skin.

"What the fuck is so funny?"

I'd answer him if I could, but I can't just yet. All I can think about is my girl, who although, thousands of miles away...

Is still up to her old Tricks.

TWENTY-ONE

I'M LOST IN THOUGHTS OF GRIM WHEN I SHOULD BE concentrating on the work in front of me. I wonder how he is. What he's doing. If he misses me as much as my heart aches for him. I love it in Ireland, but as happy as I've been here, it doesn't make me love or want to be with Grim any less, but it does complicate the situation more because now I won't just be leaving a place when the time comes.

I'll be leaving my family.

"Having troubles?" My mother asks, glancing at the empty page on my desk. Her eyes drop to the biggest complication, my large rounded stomach, or more directly, the baby growing inside. "Are you feeling ill?"

"No, I...*we* are fine. It's just that I'll never get this right," I complain, staring down at my text book. Gabby and I are both finishing our basic education courses. Soon, we will both have high school diplomas. I've found out that as excited and eager as I am to have an education, there are some subjects that give me the urge to toss the text book into the fireplace.

"It's math. No one ever gets it right," my mother says, "I'll go fix you a snack. Be back in a moment."

She passes my dad on her way out the door. I smile up at him, but his frown makes me worry. "What is it?"

"This is for you," Callum says, handing me a small box. "Came from a messenger just now."

"What is it?" I ask.

"I don't—"

I cock my head and give him a look that says *really?*

He puffs out his cheeks and blows out his breath. "Fine. Yes, I opened it. Yes, I know what is inside, and yes, most importantly, I know what it's not, which is anything that can harm you. At least, I hope not. You happy, my darling girl?"

I noticed over the last several months, that when talking to me or Gabby, or my mother, Callum, even when angry or upset, always ends his sentences with an endearment. A cushion to the blow. A reminder that he can be both upset and still love. It's one of my favorite things about him. My other is watching Callum get flustered. Not being used to having two teenage girls to care for, it's a daily occurrence that always ends in giggles from the three of us and Callum storming off in a cloud of Irish swears.

I smile. "Sort of."

I look down at the small box. Written across the top in familiar handwriting is my name. I know exactly who it's from. My heart beats wildly.

Gabby and my mother enter the room. "What is it, dear? Is it the babe? Is everything alright?"

"Everything is…" I can't finish because it's not true. Everything isn't fine. "The baby is fine," I say, pressing my flattened palm to my rounded stomach. A little hand gives me a high five and then proceeds to pummel my ribs. I wince and take a deep breath.

"What's that?" Gabby asks, pointing to the box.

"It's from Grim," I say.

"Just give her some room, and let her open the darn thing," Callum barks. But he doesn't retreat, and neither do Gabby or my mother. In fact, they all crowd in closer.

I take a deep breath and rip off the top. There's no note. No card. Just a ring. A man's ring. A simple black rose with bleeding red stones falling from the petals. I hold it up for my family to see.

Gabby smiles. My mother looks terrified.

I have no idea how to feel just yet.

I glance from the ring to Callum's stoic face. "Does this mean what I think it does?"

He rocks on his feet and clasps his hands behind his back. "Aye."

"So, Marco is…" Gabby trails off, but I know she's not upset about potentially hearing of her brother's demise. I recognize the look on her face. She's merely impatient.

Callum nods. "Yes, darling. Marco Ramos is dead. The war is over."

TWENTY-TWO

SEVERAL MONTHS LATER

CHIEF DAVID PULLS INTO THE DRIVEWAY, AND I FIND it odd, considering I haven't seen him outside the reservation save for a handful of times. He glances at the bucket of stucco in my hand. "Renovating?"

I look up to the house, shielding my eyes from the sun. "As much as I like to think the bullet holes give the old girl character, I think it's time for a fresh start." I set down the bucket on a step of the ladder and pick up a trowel and take a large scoop of the grey cement like mixture. I flick my wrist to shuck the mixture over one of the holes I'd already wired up, pressing it into the wire then smoothing it over. "Once it's dry, I'll add another layer to mimic the skip trowel texture on the non-damaged portion of the walls. She'll be good as new after a layer of fresh paint."

The chief surprises me by shrugging off his jacket and laying it across the bed of his truck. He rolls up his shirtsleeves and picks up another trowel. He digs it into the bucket and begins to repair another one of the holes.

"You don't have to help," I say.

"Did you know what I did on the reservation before the casino opened?" he asks.

"No, I don't." We work quickly together. I pick up the bucket, and Chief David helps me move the ladder a few feet to the next set of holes.

"Stucco and drywall," he says proudly. "It's tedious work. But I always enjoyed it. Kept my mind focused. I came up with some of my best and worst ideas for the tribe and my people while laboring in the heat covered in drywall dust and stucco mud."

"I can understand that," I say looking up at the house. Bedlam. I want it to be more than a house. I want it to be a home. In case... I shake the thought away and resume my work.

"I know what you're doing," the chief says. "Does she know the war is over?"

"I'm not sure. Callum knows because Marci told Alby. I don't know if he's told her, but it doesn't matter. I told her there isn't a deadline on this. I want her to want to come back, and not just because the war is over and it's safe for her now."

"She'll come. Of that, I have no doubt," the chief says, sounding sure.

"We don't know that for sure." I finish the last bullet hole, then toss my trowel in the bucket. I don't want to get my hopes up, but honestly, this entire house project is a sign that my hopes are already up. "If she does come back someday, I want to give her something to come back to."

"A home."

I nod. "Safety. Security. A life. A real one," I admit.

The chief tosses his own trowel into the bucket. "Everything. You want to give her everything."

I inspect the chief's work. It's immaculate, much better than my own. "You gonna tell me what really brought you off the rez today? I assume the trip wasn't just to help me stucco. Good work, by the way."

"Thanks, and you're right. As much as I like working with my hands, it's not the reason I'm here." He wipes his hands on a rag and adjusts his turquoise bolo tie. "The reservation lab received an odd request. Actually, I received the request personally, and then sent it over to the lab."

"Does is affect security?" I ask.

The chief retrieves his jacket. He reaches inside and retrieves a folded paper he hands to me. It's a blood work form from the lab. "No, but it affects you."

I hand him back the paper. "You've already tested my

blood, if you don't recall. Unfortunately, not a trace of the tribe. I believe your words were something along the lines of *you're the bastard son I've never wanted*."

He shakes his head and holds up his hands, refusing to take back the paper. "I know that. Read it. It's not a Native blood test."

I look it over again and realize it's not blank, although the line where a name should be is blank. There are boxes checked for two samples A and B.

"We didn't receive the actual samples, but the DNA breakdown was sent in an email," he explains.

"It's a paternity test," I say, confused.

"It is."

"Why did you get it?" I ask, as a ridiculous thought begins to unfurl in the back of my mind.

"Because we've got the best lab in the whole damn country. We can pinpoint origin down to a village or tribe or region, better than any of those mail-in tests can. And because a favor was asked of me and I figured you'd want me to oblige."

"I mean why are you showing it to me?" I glance over the paper again, but it's as jumbled as my thoughts. "Just tell me what the fuck is going on?"

"The DNA samples emailed over were of two females."

The chief has a knowing look on his lined face. "You

think Gabby and Tricks?" I shake my head. "But they already know they aren't related."

"That's what I thought at first. Maybe, they just wanted to be sure. But then the report came back. It turns out that one female is around eighteen to twenty-five years in age, consistent with Gabby, but the other unrelated female is under a year."

Love and worry and panic swirl around in my brain. I lean on the ladder for support. "A baby."

"If they compared the baby's DNA to Gabby's it means they were trying to rule out, or find out if she was related to Marco." I say as the realization takes hold.

"Yes, but since we store all of our DNA reports in our system, I told them to go the direct route and test the child against you."

The baby could be Marco's or any one of...I push the thought aside, it leaves my mind as quick as if it never was. It doesn't matter whose DNA made *our* kid. Tricks is mine; so, the baby is mine. It's just that simple. Like breathing. I don't even have to think about it. Mine. A little girl. Holy shit. I have a little girl.

"The results," he turns the page toward me.

I shove it away. "No, I don't need to know."

"Why not?"

I smile. "Because it doesn't fucking matter. I'm a dad."

"Good man." Chief David slaps me on the shoulder.

"Congratulations, Papa." He shrugs his coat back on and looks up to the house. "Looks like you've got more renovating to do than you thought."

I stand outside and look up at the house for hours without moving. I might never move again. I'm fixated on the swirling emotions inside me. I'm half-tempted to go to Ireland and drag Tricks back, even though every fiber in my being tells me it's a decision she has to make on her own, but now, she's had my baby, and I haven't heard a word from her since I sent her the ring. It's been so long. What if her feelings for me have changed? What if she doesn't want me to be part of her daughter's life?

My daughter.

That won't fucking happen.

I'll give Tricks time.

A month. Tops.

After that, I'll be going to collect what's mine.

My girls.

TWENTY-THREE

"IT CAME OUT BEAUTIFUL," MARCI SAYS, STANDING next to me on the driveway. I've just finished replacing the shutters and windows. The entire house has been repainted, and new shingles line the roof. "You did a great job."

"Thanks. Looks better than it did."

"The inside, too. Especially the one room. It's never looked better."

I shrug. "It needed a face-lift. I figured while I was already at it I'd finish the job. I should have done it a long time ago."

"I know exactly what you figured, Grim. You can't fool me." She wraps her arm around my waist. "She'll love it."

If she comes back.

It's been weeks since Callum learned of Marco's death and the end of the war. Either he hasn't told her or she doesn't want to come back. Either way, doubt has crept in shadowing my every move.

Sounds of tires on the pavement behind me. My instinct is to reach for my gun, but it's not there. There's no need for that now. The war is over. I turn around, and Marci takes a step back into the house with a ridiculous smile on her face just as a town car with blacked-out windows pulls up in front of the house.

The rear door opens and out steps Tricks. Or what used to be Tricks.

She's filled out. Muscular. More...everything. My mouth waters, and my fucking heart stops. She's wearing a pair of tight fitted faded jeans, ripped in all the right places and hugging her every curve. Her tits are bigger, straining against the thin fabric of her Debbie Gibson t-shirt that hangs haphazardly off one shoulder revealing a new tattoo I can't make out from this distance. Her hair is down and hanging wild around her face, longer than I remember, well past her shoulders now. She pushes her sunglasses from her eyes up onto her head. Her blue-green eyes are bright and clear. A mixture of a wild green lawn and the bluest of skies.

Her eyes land on me. She smiles.

I don't even know I'm moving until we meet in the middle of the lawn. For a second, I'm unsure of what I'm supposed to do. "You're here," is all I manage to say, as if I can't really believe what I'm seeing.

She smiles wickedly, then changes her expression to a pout, pushing out her bottom lip. "Mister," she begins, with a begging look in her big eyes. She rocks on the balls of her feet and produces a tiny kitten from behind her back. "I was wondering if you knew anyone who could take Mrs. Fuzzy here. She's lonely and needs a home, and I swear she'll be no trouble at all."

I laugh at my girl and go to pet the kitten, who takes a swipe at my hand.

She giggles and then remembers her act. "See? Friendly as can be." She bites her bottom lip. "So, can we keep her?"

"I think you're forgetting something about that day." I say with wicked intentions of my own.

"Oh yeah? What's that?"

"The kiss," I grab her hips and pull her close until my lips are on hers. She feels soft and warm and very much like home. The kitten meows, forcing us apart.

"So," she says. "Can we keep her?"

"We can," I say.

A throat clears, and I look up to find Callum Eagan standing at the curb with his wife who's bent over the back seat. She stands and turns around revealing a baby cradled in her arms.

My eyes go wide, and it's as if I really am meeting

Tricks for the first time all over again because whatever defenses Tricks hadn't crumbled that day shatter like glass all around me with one look at my baby girl.

Tricks squeezes my hand and leads me over to her mother. She takes the baby from her arms and places her into mine. My heart literally breaks. Pain like I've never felt and wanted more of strikes me like a dagger to the chest.

"So," Tricks says, leaning in over my shoulder to smile at our baby in my arms. "Can we keep her?"

I look down at the blonde bundle swaddled in pink. Her eyes open, and she smiles up at me with shining gold eyes.

I clear my throat. "Absofuckinglutley."

"Oh," Tricks says, "One more thing." She comes around to my front and holds up my wallet, the one that had just been in my back pocket. She waives it in the air. "You might want this back."

I laugh and look down at my baby and up to Tricks. My pocket might be empty, but my heart has never been so full.

"What's her name?" I ask.

Tricks smoothes a lock of curls from our daughter's eyes. Her gaze meets mine. She reaches out and presses her hand to the base of my throat over my Bedlam tattoo.

"Rosey."

"I HAVE SOMETHING TO SHOW YOU," Grim tells me. He tugs me by the hand into the house and opens a door across from the master bedroom. I'm so overwhelmed with emotion at what's before me that I sink to my knees while Grim rocks Rosey in his arms.

"Grim, it's beautiful," I whisper, taking in the large quote stenciled onto the soft pink wall above a pristine white crib.

> 66 *Let her sleep, for when she wakes she will move mountains.*"
>
> -ANONOMOUS

On the other side of the room is a changing table, stocked with diapers, rash cream, even nipple pads. There's a shelf above it stocked with children's books.

What has me gasping in the mural painted around the window. It's a castle with waiving pink flags at the top. Over it is a crown of flowers alternating between black, white, and pink roses.

"It's us," Grim says.

I turn back to find him staring at me. He's even better-looking than I remembered and after months apart the air in the room crackles and snaps. I can practically see it, flashing little lights exploding like firecrackers all around us.

"I know, it's...I can't believe you did all this," I say, feeling every emotion pile up inside me. "It must have taken a long time."

Grim nods. "I started the second the Chief told me about the DNA test."

I grin feeling ashamed for not having told him myself. "I knew he'd tell you. That's kind of why of all the labs I picked his. I wanted him to tell you before I had to. I'm sorry. I chickened out."

"Don't be sorry, Tricks," he says, stepping up to me. The hand not holding Rosey tips my chin up so my eyes meet his. "I understand. I wish I was there for you. It must have been hard when you found out you were pregnant."

"It was, but mostly I was worried about what you'd think of it. Of us." I wave the thought away and look to our sleeping child in his arms. "You must have been so relieved when you saw the results."

He looks to Rosey. "I'm seeing them right now, for the first time," he admits. "She has your hair and my eyes."

My heart stops. "You mean, you did all this—" I wave my arms to the walls, the beautiful white crib, the rocking chair, "—before you knew she was yours?"

He shrugs casually as if it was a totally natural reac-

tion to build a nursery and a life for a child you didn't
father. "Tricks, the second the chief told me you had a
baby, she was mine. The rest didn't matter."

"I've been obsessing all this time," I say with a sigh.

"Have a little faith in me, Trick's. I'm a monster, but
you gave me a heart, and I'm giving it back. To both of
you. She's mine. You're mine." His eyes drop to my
breasts which are at least a cup size bigger since I had
Rosey. Grim's voice deepens. "All mine."

TWENTY-FOUR

My parents and Gabby are staying at a hotel a few towns over. I saw the hesitation in my father's eyes before he left, but after having a private talk with Grim, which I'm sure included threats to his life, they reluctantly left me and Rosey with the promise to be back first thing in the morning.

"When are they going back to Ireland?" Grim asks as I step out of the shower, wearing nothing but a towel.

I'm tired from the long trip but a shirtless Grim has suddenly given me a second wind.

He's sitting on the bed, wearing a pair of tight black boxers, his back against the headboard, feet crossed at the angles. When he sees me, his lips part and his eyes darken as he takes me in. A sly smile tugs at his lips.

My body feels warm all over, and it's not from the

shower. "They're not. They refuse for us to be separated again, so they're all staying here. They're already talking about buying a house to renovate."

"It makes sense that they're staying," he says. He swings his legs over the mattress and pulls me between his spread thighs. His hands digging into my waist.

"It does?" I ask standing next to the bed.

"It does, because home is where you are." He tugs at the towel and groans, burying his nose in my belly button. He breathes me in, dragging his lips across my skin.

My arms wrap around his neck, and I yelp when he lifts me up and sets me on top of him so I'm naked, straddling his waist. His growing erection swells against my sensitive skin, and I moan at the sensation.

"Shhh...our baby might hear you," he teases.

I giggle as he lifts me with one hand, the other making quick work of the boxers in our way. When he pulls me back down, he flips me onto my back and wastes no time pressing his full lips to mine.

The heat of his throbbing erection against my skin makes me groan as he nudges my legs apart with his knees.

He kisses me deeply, parting my lips with his tongue. He rocks his hips, rubbing his cock through my wetness. I lift my hips, needing more contact. More Grim.

"I've got you, Tricks," he says against my lips. He

reaches between us and positions his thick girth at my opening, nudging the head inside, stretching me open. "We can do slow next time. Right now, I just need you."

"Yes," I moan my agreement.

He thrusts, seating himself deep inside of me. I contract around his welcome intrusion. He groans into the crook of my neck. "Fuck, Tricks. It's so good," he mumbles. "Feels so fucking good."

"Please," I hear myself beg, arching my back.

He lifts his chest from mine and reaches behind my knees, pulling my legs up over his shoulders. The position allows him even deeper inside of me. He pulls back and slams into me, his balls slapping against my ass cheeks. His eyelids are heavy as he watches my breasts bounce with every thrust with appreciation and awe. With every movement in and out he rubs against my nerve endings. It's only seconds before my lower stomach coils up so tight I'm begging for release.

"Please," I rasp again.

Grim growls and lifts my legs from my shoulders and folds my knees. Beads of sweat appear on his forehead. He presses into me again and again. "Come, Tricks. Co —
"

The way my pussy clamps around his cock silences him. I don't just come, I ascend to a height of pleasure I never knew possible. The tension releases in a spiral of pressure. A full body explosion followed by waves of sparks as I scream Grim's name, digging my fingernails into his round muscled ass cheeks.

Grim thrusts into me one final time, his neck chorded tight as I'm thrashing underneath him in the throes of the strongest orgasm I've ever known powers through me like a derailed train.

He grows impossibly hard inside of me. I feel his cock throb as he comes on a strangled groan, flooding me with his cum.

Grim collapses beside me, tucking me against his chest.

"That was—" I begin to say, but I can't find the right word in my lust addled state.

"Nothing yet," Grim interrupts with a laugh and a wicked gleam in his eyes.

For a few moments we relax in comfortable silence. After we both catch our breath, he turns on his side, propping himself up on his elbow. "We have one more thing to deal with."

"What's that?" I ask, reaching out to brush my hand over the rose tattoo on his throat.

He sighs. "Mona."

TWENTY-FIVE

My parents come over in the morning with Gabby as promised. We eat breakfast with Marci and Grim's brothers. Ma and Marci spend most of the morning passing Rosey back and forth between them, gushing over their grandchild. Callum and Grim discussed business while Sandy sits, oddly silent, glaring at Gabby from across the table when she isn't looking.

I've never felt more at peace, or more at home. It's natural, having us all here together.

Marci and Ma barely pay us any attention when we ask them to watch Rosey for a little while. They are both on the living floor clapping as Rosey crawls between them. They wave us off as if asking wasn't even necessary.

"I think they're in love," I say to Grim.

"Them and me both," he replies, tucking my hand into his, leading me to the garage. He places a helmet on my head and checks twice to make sure the clasp is snapped in properly. He sets me on his bike, and just like before, he positions me in front of him.

The ride is peaceful without the threat of flying bullets. There are people out and about. Children laughing as they play tag in an empty field beside the road.

The peace I feel is short-lived as we approach our destination.

Rollo's cabin where he's been keeping Mona since I left for Ireland. I'm surprised to find the cabin is on reservation lands.

"Rollo is a tribesman," he explains, noticing my confusion as we dismount. He takes my helmet from me and sets it on the seat.

"I don't know what I'm going to say to her. Or what I'm going to decide," I admit to Grim as we stand on the porch. The front door is open, but the screen door in front of it is closed.

Grim raps on the aluminum with his fist. "You'll know once you see her, and if you don't, nothing has to be decided today. This is your call to make. I've been waiting for you to come back to make it, but just know that nothing has to be decided today."

When no one comes to the door, Grim tugs on my

hand, and we head to the back of the cabin where we find Rollo and Mona, naked. Mona's riding Rollo on a plastic lounge chair right there on the back porch, his fingers digging into her hips, his eyes closed and his mouth open in ecstasy.

"What the fuck?" Grim grates.

Rollo's and Mona's heads snap to us. Rollo pushes Mona off of him, protectively shielding her with his large, naked body.

Grim

"Go put some clothes on," Rollo orders Mona, who rushes inside the house.

Tricks turns around while Rollo stands and pulls on a pair of basketball shorts. A few seconds later, Mona appears again, this time wearing an oversized black t-shirt to her knees. She looks frightened. I can see her lower lip trembling from where we stand more than twenty feet away.

They descend the steps and approach us. Rollo tucks Mona under his arm, not like he's delivering a prisoner, but like he's protecting her. "What the fuck is going on, Rollo?" I growl.

"Boss, I love and respect you, but I won't turn her into you." He hugs her tighter to his big body. "She's mine."

"No, she's a prisoner of Bedlam," I remind him. "And up until this very moment, you were my soldier. A loyal one."

"She's not a Bedlam prisoner anymore. She's my wife. The tribal council—"

"She's what?" I ask, genuinely shocked. I ball my fists. Rage burns in my throat. "Rollo, the bitch is a master manipulator. You don't think she's conned you into falling for her? That it's all part of her plan to stay alive?"

"Oh, she tried to manipulate me. I almost killed her for it, too." He looks down to an apologetic-looking Mona. "Almost."

I try reasoning with him instead of beating sense into his thick skull. "It's all bullshit, Rollo. Use your head. It's not too late. Turn the bitch over, and let her suffer the consequences of her actions against Bedlam. Your *family*."

"She's my family now, too. I'd never go against Bedlam, but I'm hoping you'll side with me on this, and I won't have to." Rollo stands straight, widening his stance defensively, ushering Mona behind him. "Don't ask me to kill her. I won't do it."

"Fine, then I'll get Sandy to do it," I say through gritted teeth.

"Then, I have to remind you that I'm of tribal blood. I'm under the protection of the tribe, and now, so is

Mona. You can't harm her. If you don't believe me, ask the chief."

"That's why you married her," I groan. "Rollo, you do realize what she's done? To Tricks? To my family? To her own fucking sister? Do you know who it is you're actually fucking protecting? Because I don't think you do."

"He knows everything," Mona says, choking up. "Every horrible detail."

"And she's made amends, more so than you asked of her. She was your bait and almost your human sacrifice. Does that mean anything to you?" Rollo asks. "You're ruthless, Grim. I know that. But I also know that your black heart beats, and as you've said, I've been a loyal soldier for years. I've never questioned Belly's leadership or yours. Not once. I've fought for you. I've killed for you. I'm asking for this one thing in return. Let me deal with her. Let me take her away from Lacking. You won't ever have to see her again."

"Which means you'll never see your brothers again. Is that what you want?" I ask, growing frustrated.

Rollo looks pained.

"Why didn't you just come to me before?" I yell.

"I was waiting to see how it played out," he responds then shakes his head. Maybe, I thought over time you'd just forget about her."

I raise my eyebrows.

He blows out a breath. "Fuck, I don't know. Maybe I

didn't feel like I had a choice. Maybe..." he looks to Mona. "Maybe, I just didn't want to face it all before we had to."

"We?" I ask with a laugh, although nothing about this situation is funny. "There was a choice, and you've obviously already made it. And it was the wrong one. This decision wasn't even yours to make. It was Bedlam's, and more than that, it was hers." I point to an uncharacteristically quiet Tricks standing beside me, observing Rollo and Mona.

Tricks sighs and looks to Rollo. "Thank you."

Rollo frowns, looking as confused as I feel. "For what? I half-expected you to stab me."

"Same," I offer, raising my eyebrows at my girl, who looks anything other than angry. She looks...relieved.

Tricks exhales. "I never wanted to decide if Mona lives or dies. Rollo, you've taken the decision out of my hands. So again, thank you." She seems lighter, relieved of the burden of the choice. I feel suddenly guilty for not realizing how hard this has been on her. My simple, brutish mind thought an eye for an eye and the decision an easy one, regardless of a past connection. But to Tricks, there is nothing easy about it.

I'm about to tell her as much when she speaks again. This time to Mona. "But I can't have you stay in Lacking, or anywhere near me or my family. At least, not anytime soon. I don't want you to be separated from your brothers, but I need time. Space." She looks to Mona. "I appreciate what you've done for us, but forgiveness isn't something I'm capable of where you're concerned. At least, not right now. But I do hope you find everything you're looking for. I hope you truly change and take this second chance for what it is. A second chance." Tricks steps up to Mona. "Because if this is all bullshit—"

"I'll kill her myself," Rollo says. "You have my word, but it isn't bullshit. And I hope you do forgive her, and maybe someday, we can come back."

"I hope that, too," Tricks says, taking a step back from the confusing as fuck couple.

Rollo wraps his meaty arm around Mona and tips his chin to me before they walk off into the darkness.

"The men will think I'm weak if I let Rollo get away with betraying us like this," I say to Tricks.

"Do you think I'm weak for being grateful not to have to decide on someone's life?"

"No, I think you're the strongest person I've ever met," I tell her, brushing her lips with mine.

She smiles, and I know a quote is coming next.

> *The weak can never forgive. Forgiveness is the attribute of the strong.*

— GHANDI

TWENTY-SIX

I'm helping Marci at the brothel while Grim and Callum are out looking at potential houses for my parents to purchase. Ma is in the Bedlam living area, watching over Rosey while I sit at the reception desk, attempting to make sense of the computer system.

"We need a proper receptionist," I tell Marci as she enters the room with a pile of clean sheets in her hand. "The appointment system isn't being used properly, if at all. I look down at the calendar on the desk where the girls have been handwriting in appointments instead of entering them into the system. "We can't properly keep track of accounting unless it's in the system."

"I've put an ad out for one, but it's harder to find someone to work the front desk than it is to find girls willing to work in the back." She sets the stack of linens down on the counter.

Erin, one of the Irish temps, walks through the door with a bright smile on her face.

Erin, as well as several other of the Irish girls, chose to stay at the brothel once the violence ended. Which was great for the business because not a lot of the women who worked here previously had come back as promised. Between the few women who did come back, and the Irish girls who stayed, we were now fully operational, save for a qualified receptionist.

"Hey Erin, you don't by chance know of qualified receptionist, do you?" I ask.

"I used to be a secretary in Ireland a few years back."

"You did?" Marci asks.

Erin nods. "I did. I ran an office of over fifty employees. I'd be more than happy to fill in for a while until you find someone, and I can help train them if you'd like, but I make too much in the back to sit up front full time."

"Thank you," I say. "That would be amazing."

Erin smiles cheerfully. "I've got to go set up my room. I've got a regular coming in a few minutes."

"I'll let you know when he arrives," I tell her.

With a smile, Erin heads down the hall. Marci picks up her stack of linens once more and follows.

The bell above the door rings. I'm expecting it to be Erin's appointment, but that's not who I find standing before me. My jaw drops when a woman steps tentatively inside and sets down a cardboard box beside her.

"Leo!" I shout, leaping from the desk, knocking down the chair in the process. I round the counter and throw my arms around her.

Leo is silent except for a few soft sobs.

"Leo, what's wrong? What happened?" I ask, pulling back from her. I keep my hands on her forearms as she looks at me with tear stained eyes.

Leo's stained black tank top has a severe tear down the seams under her arm, exposing the curve of her right breast. Her denim shorts are worn and filthy. In place of a button, they're being held together with a shoestring. Leo's a thin girl, but now she's downright emaciated. Her shoulder bones are sharp. Her clavical pronounced. Her sad eyes are sunken like a skull, surrounded by deep dark circles. Tears, both fresh and old, stain her dirt-smudged cheeks.

Using her eyes, Leo points to the cardboard box beside her.

I peer inside, gasping at the contents. An infant, swaddled in a newspaper. "You had a baby!" I exclaim.

One of the things about being a mother is the incorrect assumption that you somehow have the authority to touch other people's children because we are all part of the same club, and we all need a little help now and again. I don't even think before reaching for the infant, cradling it in my arms. "Shit," I look to Leo, "I didn't ask. Is this alright?"

She nods, smoothing back the child's thick dark hair.

The baby cries out; its face reddens. I offer it my finger. The baby wraps a chubby little hand around it, pulling it toward his face, he sucks the tip of my finger into its mouth.

"He's hungry," Leo whispers.

"Do you want a private room to feed him?" I offer.

She shakes her head and looks to the floor in shame. Her voice trembles. "I...I can't. I'm polluted. I was clean for a while, but I ..." her eyes water. "I fucked up and..."

"Shhhh," I tell her. "Come with me."

I call out to Marci that I'm stepping away from the desk. She shouts back that she'll be up in a minute.

Leo follows me as I lead her to the private door that leads to the Bedlam living area. I punch in my code and push open the door.

My ma stands from the recliner when she sees us come in. Her eyes look to Leo and then to the crying baby in my arms.

"What do we have here?" she asks.

"Ma, this is my friend Leo. She was with me at the Los Muertos compound. One of the only people to show me kindness. Leo, this is my mother."

"Your..." Leo's eyes widen.

"Yes, my mother," I say proudly. "Trust me. Your

shock is nothing compared what mine was when I learned of her."

"Holy shit," Leo swears, covering her mouth. "You could be twins."

"That's very kind of you Leo, but I've got some crows feet that might argue with that observation," my mom says, brushing off the compliment, but she's unable to hide the delight in her eyes, and I know for a fact she loves when people tell her how much we look alike.

My mother stands before me and rubs the back of her finger along the baby's cheek. "And who is this beautiful wee thing?"

"This is Leo's baby…"

"Jack," Leo finishes. "His name is Jack."

My mother smiles. "He's lovely. What's wrong, little dear?" she coos. "Are ye hungry?"

I don't miss Leo's wince.

"Ma, can you do me a big favor and run to the reservation store and grab Jack some formula?" I ask.

"Not a problem. I was going to wait until Rosey woke from her nap before heading over there myself for a few necessities, but now that you're here to mind her, I'll pop over and be right back in a gif."

I appreciate the lie for Leo's sake. Ma was just at that store a few hours ago stocking up in items for the Bedlam fridge. "Thank you," I say.

"Think nothing of it. It won't be a bother." She grabs

her purse.

After she leaves I guide Leo over to the couch.

Jack's wailing grows louder.

The store is only fifteen minutes away by car, but thinking of Jack going another thirty minutes without food heightens my maternal anxiety as my heart breaks for both him and Leo.

"You had a baby," Leo whispers, looking over at Rosey's portable crib where my baby is fast asleep, clutching her little white blanket, filling the room with the sweet sound of baby snores.

"I did," I say over Jack's cries. Suddenly, I feel wet. "I think little Jack peed on me," I say lifting him from my lap.

"No, I don't think that's it." Leo stares at my chest where two big wet spots have leaked through my bra and t-shirt.

"It's because he's crying," I explain. "Rosey's cries always set them off like this."

Jacks little face contorts with unhappiness. His trembling lips expose little red angry gums underneath.

I look at Leo. I don't want to offend her, but I can't take it anymore. I have to do something. "Would you mind if I.." I start, but stop and start again. "Rosey's not awake yet to feed, and it would be a more of a favor to me because it's ridiculously painful if they're full for too long."

"Oh please. Please do," Leo says, her words filled with relief. "Thank you."

I lift my shirt and unsnap my bra. It takes little Jack a moment to realize what's going on, but after a few moments and some hushed words of encouragement from both Leo and myself, he finally takes my nipple in his mouth. His screams replaced with the sound of soft sucks and swallows that sound like little sighs of relief.

"I don't know what to do," Leo says, watching her baby eat. "I came here because I've got nowhere to go." She plants her face in her hands. "EJ, I know it's a lot to ask, but..." her voice cracks. "Do you think you can take Jack? Just for a while until I can get my shit together. I've got to get clean. Get a job. Find a place for us to live."

"Do you know who the father is?" I ask, keeping my question judgment free. After all, there was a time when I didn't know who Rosey's father was either.

She shakes her head.

"Where have you been living?" I ask.

"On the streets," she admits with a sniffle. "Here and there. I've been selling myself trying to keep Jack fed and buy diapers. I mean, it's no different than what I was doing at Los Muertos, except maybe better because I'm getting paid, but worse because now I've got nowhere to go. When I started to show Marco threatened to sell the baby on the black market once it was born. I couldn't bear the thought. I ran. When Los Muertos collapsed, I thought I could go back to the compound and live with some of the people there. But everyone was gone. It was gone. The city tore the whole thing down."

"I know, I'm sorry," I say. "Not that it's gone, but that you're in this situation."

I look down to baby Jack. He's unlatched and fast asleep, milk spilling from the side of his open mouth. "He's milk drunk," I say.

I hand Jack over to Leo while I re-clasp my bra and tug down my shirt. I stand and take Jack once more, carrying him over to the changing table where I lay him down. Carefully, and quietly, I remove the newspaper he's wrapped in and clean him the best I can with baby wipes. I change him into a fresh diaper that's a little too big but will make do for now. I wrap him in a fresh white swaddling blanket.

Leo forces a sad smile. "So will you? Will you take him?" Her knee bounces beneath her folded hands.

"I'll do you one better," I offer. Returning to the couch, I place baby Jack back into his mother's arms.

Leo raises her eyebrows in question.

I smile at my old friend and take her hand in mine. "I'll take you both."

WHEN I ARRIVE BACK at the house, Grim is already there. I tell him about Leo and how I've given her a room at the brothel for her and her son until I can find her something more permanent. The girls there were all over the moon to have a baby to fawn over. And Ma stayed back for a while to help Leo and little Jack get settled in.

Grim goes one step further and insists on sending a home-rehab specialist to help Leo get clean. I take his hand in mine. "Thank you."

He shrugs. "She was good to you. It's nothing."

"To me, it's everything," I tell him. "And, after she's clean, I'd like to train her for the receptionist position." I tell him. "If it's okay with you. Marci already agreed and we have someone to train her."

"I think it's a great idea," he says, kissing me on the forehead. I place Rosey in her crib and turn off the light. Carefully, Grim shuts the door behind us.

We silently creep back into the living room and are surprised to find the Chief and Margaret, waiting for us.

"Welcome back," the chief offers, standing and opening his arms.

I haven't seen him since in the weeks since I've gotten back, and hadn't realized how much I missed him until now. I run into his arms for a big, bear hug. He smells like spicy cologne and fresh air.

Margaret places a hand on my back. "Congratulations. I heard you didn't come home empty-handed."

"Thank you," I say to her, releasing the chief, who offers Grim a congratulations of his own with a handshake and a slap on the back.

"I have to ask," Grim says to the chief, and I know what's coming next. "Did you marry Rollo and Mona?"

The chief nods. "I did. And it's binding and legal. Water jug ritual, blanket binding, in front of the whole tribe. It's done."

"'Wait," I say as the memory of the ritual he performed on Grim and myself comes back to me. "Did you say water jug ritual and blanket binding?"

The chief swallows hard as I approach him slowly.

Margaret suppresses a laugh by covering her mouth with her hand.

I point an accusing finger at his chest. "Tell me, chief, do you use those two rituals in anything other than a wedding ceremony?"

He grimaces.

Margaret's laughter breaks. She falls onto the couch in damn near hysterics.

"Is there?" I press.

He looks to Grim who doesn't appear nearly as surprised as I am.

The Chief finally answers. "I...no, no there is not."

"So then —" I begin.

The Chief's smile is blinding and unapologetic. "You and Grim. You're married."

TWENTY-SEVEN

ONE MONTH LATER...

THE CEREMONY IS THE SAME AS IT HAD BEEN LAST time, yet everything else is different. This time, I walk down an aisle to Grim linked arm-and-arm with both of my parents. The chief conducts the ceremony in English, and we are very aware of what is taking place, the promises we're making to each other. Also, we are dressed for the occasion this time around. Grim looks breathtaking in a black button-down shirt, dark black pants, and his usual clean white sneakers. I opted for a long, strapless, black maxi dress. I'm carrying a bouquet of black roses, a matching crown of which is weaved into my hair. Marci takes them from me as Grim takes my hands in his. The biggest difference of all is the golden-eyed, curly headed toddler sucking on her thumb between our legs.

"Da da da da daaaaaaa!" She pulls on Grim's pants.

"Shhhhh, Rosey," Grim coos.

Rosey looks up at him. Her pink, heart-shaped lips spread into a smile, revealing two different sized white squares lodged into her upper gums.

Grim's smile spreads. He looks from her to me. My heart and stomach flutter. I'm awash in a wave of emotion. The strength of it stronger than chains, unbreakable by any man. What makes those chains even stronger are the additional links that Rosey has added. Our connection grows stronger every day, and it's not just between the two of us now, but three. I never thought I could love Grim more, but seeing him love our child and feeling that love between them makes me feel complete in a way I've never thought was possible.

"You may kiss your bride," Chief David concludes. Grim's gaze darkens as he pulls me into his arms and plants a kiss to my lips that lasts for much longer than would be appropriate, but the crowd around us doesn't seem to mind, as our friends, family, and all of Bedlam clap, whoop, and whistle.

"I present to you, Mr. and Mrs. Tristan Paine," Chief David announces proudly. We separate when Rosey pushes our legs apart. Grim laughs and bends over to pick her up. His free hand holds tightly onto mine.

Haze steps to the front of the crowd. "The King and Queen of Bedlam!" He presses his closed fist to his heart.

"My life!" he roars loudly. The rest of the crowd joins them, including Grim and myself, and even Rosey, who balls her fist and places it against her dad's chest, babbling along "My death. My honor. My loyalty. For Bedlam. For Brotherhood. For Always."

We walk through the cheering crowd, who throws seeds into the air as we pass. Grim covers Rosey's head with his hand to protect her. Once we are clear, Marci walks over to us. "I'm so proud of both of you." She says with tears in her eyes. "Belly would be, too." She waves away her tears and leans down to our little girl, taking her hand. "Rosey, you want to come play with Grandma Marci?"

Rosey giggles, leaping from Grim's arms and into Marci's. She plants a kiss on our little girl's head and adjusts her matching crown of roses before carrying her off.

Callum approaches us. He kisses both of my cheeks and shakes Grim's hand. Grim tries to pull his hand back but my father doesn't release him. "Grim, it goes without saying that if you do anything to break my little girl's heart that I'm going to break every fucking bone in your body."

"Da," I groan.

Much to my surprise Grim doesn't get angry. Instead, he smiles and claps his hand on Callum's shoulder. "I'd expect nothing less, sir."

"Good, now, where's my grand baby?" he asks, releasing Grim's hand.

I point to Marci who's bouncing Rosey on her knee. Ma is beside them, making faces at our little girl who giggles and reaches out her little hand, tugging on Ma's nose.

Callum makes a beeline for the group and joins them in fawning over Rosey who eats up the attention.

"She is going to be so spoiled," Grim says with a chuckle.

"More importantly, she is going to be so loved," I reply.

"Her childhood will be so different from ours," Grim says.

"Thank fucking god for that," I say. "Although, if it wasn't for our shitty childhoods, I might never have met you."

Grim scrunches his nose and wraps his arms around me. "Not true. I would have found my way to you eventually. I'll always find my way to you." He brushes his lips over mine sending a shiver up my spine.

He pulls away tugs me from the crowd. We walk past the reception area where a band is set up in the corner. Picnic benches sit under a series of banyan trees, complete with strings of twinkle lights floating between. In the center of the tables are small bouquets of black, pink, and white roses in mason jar vases.

Once we're concealed to the crowd behind a thick trunk of one of the trees, Grim cups my chin. "Hello, wife," he says with a sheepish grin. He presses his lips to mine, then brushes them along my jaw. "I've been waiting to say that to you for so long now."

I raise an eyebrow. "You mean the past thirty-seconds?"

His dark eyes are gleaming with wickedness. "No, since the first time we were married."

"You knew!" I say, playfully pushing at his chest.

Grim holds my wrists against him, pulling me closer. "I knew. When the chief wanted to do the ritual, I..."

"You're the one who told him which ritual..."

"I did. You were mine. Since that very first day you conned me into taking your pussy...cat." He releases one of my wrists and snakes his hand around to the back of my neck, kneading his fingers seductively into my flesh. "It was only fair. A trick for a trick."

"You mean a trick for a Tricks," I correct him, leaning into his touch.

"Exactly. Although you aren't just Tricks now. You're Imogen Parish Egan Paine." He chuckles. "Is that what you've decided? Did I get it all right?"

I nod and trail my hand along the stubble of his jaw. My thumb over his full bottom lip, which he kisses. "It's who I am. I'm not just one thing. One name. I'm all of them." I smile. "Besides, Queen of England was taken."

"You're my queen." He kisses my lips, and I open my mouth to him. "You're my everything," he mumbles against my mouth. "Mine. Now and forever."

"I'm yours, body and soul," I whisper.

"I love you, Imogen Parish Egan Paine. I'm your possession as much as you are mine. I belong to you. My love. My life. My honor. My loyalty. For always."

Someone coughs behind us.

Grim doesn't release me. He keeps me in his arms, turning us both to face Sandy.

"What?" Grim snaps, but he can't help the smile on his face.

"Uh, there's like a hundred people here that are waiting for the bride and groom to make an appearance. As entertaining as I am, it's not me they're here for."

Grim mumbles under his breath. He drapes his arm around me as we head toward the picnic tables under the stars and twinkling lights.

I spot Haze and Gabby dancing together. He releases her as the song ends, and giggling at something he says as the two of them step off the makeshift dance floor. Sandy makes a b-line toward her, tugging her to the back of the crowd where he lowers his head to hers, whispering something in her ear. Gabby takes a step back, her face heated with rage. She juts out a hip and points a finger into his chest.

"What the hell do you think is going on there?" I ask.

"I'm not sure I want to know," Grim replies. "I'm focused on something else entirely." He looks me over from my head to my toes, heating me with his gaze as he pulls me onto the dance floor. His lips are at my ears. "Marci and your ma are going to watch Rosey, tonight. After everyone is good and drunk, I'm going to steal you away. I have plans for you tonight." He pulls me into his chest, and I can feel the outline of his plans against my stomach. I gasp at the sensation. "All fucking night."

My face and body heat with anticipation. I smile up at him as the music begins to play. He pulls me closer and searches my eyes eagerly as we sway along to the soft melody. I swallow hard and nod, unable to find the words.

Lacking is no longer a perversion of a town but is well on the way to becoming what a town should be. Not just a place, but a community. Just as we are now a family, a real one.

I belong to Grim. Not because he took me. Or forced me. But because I belong to him in the same way he belongs to me.

Being someone's possession makes you nothing.

Giving yourself to someone completely makes you everything.

And that's what we do. What we'll always do. Give ourselves to one another completely.

With love, passion, and permission.

EPILOGUE

FOURTEEN MONTHS LATER

CALLUM AND AILEEN BOUGHT A THREE-STORY HOUSE in Lacking. Actually, they bought an entire block of homes they are remodeling and renovating into one massive compound, as well as the thirty acres of forest behind it that butt up the reservation. They are doting grandparents. Callum is still the head of Clan Egan but has plans to turn the operation over to Alby and retire within the next few years.

They still travel to Ireland every few months, but when I tell Ma that I feel bad for taking them away from their home, she assures me that home is where her family is, and right now, her home is in Lacking.

Even though I decided to live with Grim, Callum and Aileen's big house isn't empty as Gabby happily lives with them. We've both received our GED's and attend classes at the community college three days a week. Gabby takes a variety of classes, unsure of what she wants to do with her life. I'm enrolled in the creative writing program.

Grim and I live in the remodeled Bedlam house. Marci has moved into Grim's outside bedroom, but it's no longer just a shed made into a room, but a full apartment for her, complete with large master bath and newly added kitchen and living area. Sandy and Haze still occupy the two bedrooms upstairs, while Grim and I have taken over the master bedroom downstairs and the other bedroom across the hall, which is now Rosey's nursery.

After spending so much time apart, we're all together often. There are big family dinners at least once a week, either at my parent's house or ours with all of us. Marci, Sandy, and Haze included. Sometimes, a few of Grim's other brothers come by for the meal. Chief David and Margaret come by as much as they can. Things are going well for them. I know this because of the huge diamond Margaret has been sporting on a very important finger. And the googly eyes they make at each other when they think no one is looking.

Aileen, Marci, and I have started a clean-up committee to help those residents who can't afford to fix up their properties. We spend a lot of time with the men of Bedlam patching up bullet holes and painting over graffiti at various homes and businesses throughout Lacking. All of the gang signs in town have been removed, including Bedlam's.

Not because they aren't proud of who they are. Their Bedlam Brotherhood pride reads loud and clear on the patches of their clothes and inked into their skin, but because their black bleeding rose shouldn't instill terror in the residents.

All that's left of Bedlam's graffiti are the massive murals, works of art representing those who've fallen or the way the people felt in this town while it was under attack.

The art in the town is not to be feared any longer. It's to be appreciated.

The blood stains have been cleaned up as best they could be. Only shadows of rusty red remain splattered on the sidewalks and streets.

A ghostly reminder of what once was.

Grim rules the Bedlam Brotherhood with an iron fist and a full heart. There is happiness at every corner, overshadowing the occasional dark reminders of the past.

"Is this it?" Grim asks, eying the box on my lap, the one I've yet to open.

"It is," I answer, rubbing my palm over the taped seam.

Grim takes his knife from his pant leg and cuts open

the box on my lap. My mouth drops open as if he's just cut the clothes from my body.

"What?" he asks. "You may not know this, but staring at a box doesn't open it."

"I'm just nervous."

"I'm not," he says, crouching before me. "I'm excited. You haven't let me read a single page. I don't even know the fucking title." He opens the cardboard flaps. "The suspense is killing me, Tricks."

I reach in and pull the packing from the box, setting it beside me on the couch. I glance down and am immediately filled with happiness and pride. I've worked so hard on this book. After long days of caring for Rosey and attending classes, I'd spend even longer nights filled with doubt and staring at a blank page on my laptop and blinking cursor, mocking my ability to put my story into words. But I did it. And here, in my hands, is the product of that labor and love.

I pick up the first book from the stack and hand it to Grim.

He turns it over, revealing the simple black cover with a shadowed hood looming over the white lettering. The corner of his lip twitches. "Holy shit," he says. "I knew you were writing a story based on your life story, but this...wow. You're incredible. So fucking incredible."

"Do you like the title?" I ask.

He nods as he runs his fingers over the raised letting. There's pride in his voice as he reads it out loud.

"Nothing's Fair in Love and Gang War."

EPILOGUE CONTINUED

I follow Tricks, lurking far enough behind so she won't notice me but close enough I can see very well what she's doing. And what she's been doing both makes me want to laugh and wrap my hands around her throat. All the while, my chest swells with something that feels a lot like pride. While my cock swells with something else entirely.

She started out by pickpocketing a man in a suit. She leaned over to pick something up, knowing full well he was going to look down her shirt. She'd swiped his phone and wallet out of his briefcase before the mother-fucker had a chance to adjust the crotch of his pants.

She then does something that surprises me. She circles the slot machines on the outside of the room, pretending to be interested in a penny slot machine for a while before making her way back to the same man who she'd just taken his wallet from. The man is now confused and searching frantically for his missing items.

"Is this yours?" she says to him, playing up her southern accent and big smile. "I found it over by the slot machines and the photo on the ID looks a lot like you."

"Oh my god. Thank you. Thank you so much," he says, wiping the beaded sweat from his forehead with a handkerchief from his pocket.

"It's no problem at all. It's all in there," she says when he opens it to inspect to see if his cash is missing. "I found it lodged under the machine, so I don't think anyone else saw it but me."

"Can I buy you a drink? As a thank you," the man says, standing up and tucking his wallet away.

"No, thank you. I mean, I'd love to, but I'm just here applying for a much-needed job. Fingers crossed," she says, lifting her shoulders to her jaw and crossing her fingers on both hands. "I got a couple of kids at home and a babysitter I can't afford to pay more than the one hour. So, I gotta hurry."

She only makes it a couple of steps, but I see that by the third she's already slowed her stride, just in time for the man to shout, "Miss. Wait. I'm so stupid. Here." He takes out his wallet and hands her a few twenty-dollar bills. "Thank you again. I hope this will help pay for the babysitter."

She smiles, and she's good. Better than I ever realized. "Awe. This is so sweet. Thank you so much. This won't quite pay the sitter, but maybe, it will pay for a ride home so I won't have to take the bus since I have to see Daddy at the hospital on the way home."

He digs back into his wallet and pulls out every bill in it. "Here, take it all. For the kids."

"What kids?" she asks cheerily, tucking the now folded bills into her bra and prancing away on the balls of her feet like a newborn deer out for a frolic. Now, she's just fucking with him. I hold my hand over my mouth to suppress a laugh.

The man is left scratching his head for several minutes before heading to the ATM to refill his now empty wallet.

When I feel her presence behind me, I don't turn around. "You've gotten better."

"You haven't. I knew you were following me since I left the house."

"I was curious what you were up to," I say turning around to where she's standing so close I can smell her perfume. Every man instinct in me is shouting to shove her between two slot machines, hike up her skirt, and push inside her.

"Well, we are in a casino, and by the looks of it, I'm up about..." She pulls the money from her bra and counts it before tucking it back in. "Three hundred and forty dollars."

"What are you going to do with all that money?" I ask, raising a brow.

She raises her arms and wraps them around my neck. "Rosey's piggy bank of course," she says.

"Chief David is going to be pissed," I tell her.

She doesn't seem the least bit concerned. "Nah, he knows what I'm up to. I've been waving at him through the security cameras for weeks. Plus, he was over the moon happy when I gave him a signed copy of my book. He thinks because I mention him in it that he's super famous now."

It's true, the Chief even went so far as to make Tricks's book available at the casino gift shop.

"Speaking of Rosey, are you ready to go home, or do you have a few more *tricks* in you, tonight?" I ask.

She wags her eyebrows suggestively. Her voice is smooth and seductive. "Oh, baby, I'm done here, but I've always got a few more *tricks* for you."

I groan at the implication, pick her up, haul her over my shoulder and carry her out of the casino. Slapping her ass as she laughs wildly.

"Are we going home?" She laughs as I set her over my bike.

"Yes. Where I'm going to let you show me those tricks, and hopefully, it will end in you giving me another baby."

"Another?" she asks.

I nod and press my lips to hers. "Yes, I want another, and it's all your fault."

"My fault?" she asks, pushing against my chest.

I hold her still. "Yours. You planted this love thing inside me and now it's grown out of control. I need more people to give it to before I explode."

She gasps and looks over her shoulder, spying the Bedlam compound. "Why wait until we get home? I can show you my tricks right now."

I pick her up again and carry her toward the compound. When we reach the door, I slide her off my shoulder slowly so I can feel every inch of her gorgeous flesh against me. She unbuckles my jeans while I lift of her skirt. I feel between her legs. She's so wet and ready. I lift her off her feet, toss her down onto the couch and cover her body with my own, filling her pussy with one hard thrust. She cries out as I fuck her hard. At the end of each thrust, when her eyes roll back into her head with pleasure I recite my Bedlam Oath, telling her how much I love her in the best way I know how. "My Life." Thrust. "My Death." Thrust. "My Honor." Thrust. She cries out. I'm barely holding on. "My Loyalty." Thrust. "For you." Thrust. "For us." Thrust. She comes violently, squeezing my cock mercilessly. I push into her one last time. My balls seize and pleasure rips down my spine as I empty my cock inside her tight pussy.

We collapse together, breathing hard. She turns and

smiles up at me, and my heart seizes, shaking my body more violently than the orgasm. She brushes her lips against mine and finishes the oath.

"For always."

THE END

A PREVIEW OF KING

KING

On the day I was released from prison I found myself tattooing a pussy on a pussy. The animal onto the female part.

A cat on a cunt.

Fucking ridiculous.

The walls of my makeshift tattoo shop pulsed with the heavy beat of the music coming from my homecoming party raging on the floor below. It shook the door as if someone were rhythmically trying to beat it down. Spray paint and posters covered the walls from floor to ceiling, casting a layer of false light over everything within.

The little dark haired bitch I worked on was moaning like she was getting off. I'm sure she was rollin' because there was no way a tattoo directly above her clit could be anything other than fucking painful.

Back in the day, I could zone out for hours while tattooing, finding that little corner of my life that didn't involve all the bullshit I had to deal with on a daily basis.

In the past when I'd been locked up, albeit for much shorter periods of time, the first thing on my mind was pussy and a party. But this time the first thing I did when I walked through the door was pick up my tattoo gun, but it wasn't the same. I couldn't reach that place of temporary reprieve no matter how hard I tried. It didn't help that the tattoos people requested were getting dumber and fucking dumber.

Football team logos, quotes from books you know they've never read, and wannabe gangsters wanting teardrops on their faces. In prison, the teardrop tattoo represented taking a life. Some of the little bitches who wanted them looked like they couldn't step on a roach without cowering in the corner and crying for their mamas.

But since the majority of time my clients paid in favors and consisted mostly of bikers, strippers, and the occasional rich kid who found himself on the wrong side of the causeway, I should've lowered the bar on my expectations.

But then again it was good to be home. Actually, it

was good to be anywhere that didn't smell like vomit and wasted lives.

My own life had been moving forward at nothing short of full fucking speed ahead ever since the day I'd met Preppy. I'd loved living outside the law. I fed off the fear in the eyes of those who crossed me. The only thing I'd ever regretted was getting caught.

When I wasn't locked up, I'd spent almost every single day of the twenty-seven years I'd been on the earth in Logan's Beach, a little shit town on the gulf coast of Florida. A place where the residents on one side of the causeway lived solely to cater to the rich who lived on the other side, in high-rise beachfront condos and mansions. Trailer parks and run down houses less than a mile from the kind of wealth it takes more than one generation to accumulate.

On my eighteenth birthday, I bought a run-down stilt home hidden behind a wall of thick trees, on three acres of land that practically sat under the bridge. In cash. And along with my best friend Preppy, we moved on up to the rich side of town like the white trash version of the motherfucking Jeffersons.

True to our words, we became our own men and answered to no one. We did what we wanted. I turned my drawing into tattooing.

Preppy got bitches.

I fucked. I fought. I partied. I got wasted. I stole. I

fucked. I tattooed. I sold dope. I sold guns. I stole. I fucked. I made fucking money.

And I fucked.

There wasn't a party I didn't like or that didn't like me. There wasn't a chick who didn't give me the go-ahead move, lifting her hips so I could slide off her panties. I got that shit every single fucking time.

Life wasn't just good. Life was fucking great. I was on top of the fucking world and no one fucked with me or mine.

No one.

And then it all changed and I spent three years in a tiny windowless cell, studying the changing cracks in the concrete block walls.

When I was done with the purple cartoon cat, I applied salve, covered it with wrap, and disposed of my gloves. Did this girl think that guys would be turned on by this thing? It was good work, especially since I'd been out of commission for three years, but it was covering up my favorite part of a woman. If I undressed her and saw it, I would flip her over.

Which sounded like a good idea. Getting laid would help shake this post prison haze and I could get back to the things that used to be important to me without this lingering sense of dread looming in my conscious.

Instead of sending the girl back out to the party I roughly grabbed her and yanked her down the table toward me. I stood, flipping her over onto her stomach. With one hand on the back of her neck, I pushed her head down onto the table, releasing my belt buckle with the other. I grabbed a condom from the open drawer.

She knew beforehand that money wasn't the type of currency I was looking for, and I didn't do free. So I lined up the head of my cock and took her pussy as payment for her new tattoo. Of a pussy.

Fuck my life.

The girl had a great body, but after a few minutes of irritating over-the-top moaning, she wasn't doing anything for me. I could feel my cock going soft inside her. This wasn't supposed to be happening, especially not even after years of my right hand and my imagination being my only sexual partners.

What the fuck is wrong with me?

I grabbed her throat with both hands and squeezed, picking up my pace, taking out my frustrations with each rough thrust in rhythm with the heavy beat from the other room.

Nothing.

I was about to pull out and give up.

I almost didn't notice the door opening.

Almost.

Staring up from my doorway was a vacant pair of doll-like blue eyes framed by long icy-blonde hair, a small dimple in the middle of her chin, a frown on her full pink lips. A girl, no older than seventeen or eighteen, a bit skinny.

A bit haunted.

My cock stirred to life, dragging my attention back to the fact that I was still pumping into the brunette. My orgasm hit me hard, spiraling up my spine and taking me by complete surprise. I closed my eyes, blowing my load into pussy tattoo, collapsing onto her back.

What the fuck?

By the time I opened my eyes again, the door was closed and girl with the sad eyes was gone.

I'm fucking losing my mind.

I rolled out of and off the brunette who was luckily still breathing, although unconscious from either strangulation or the dope that had made her pupils as big as her fucking eye sockets.

I sat back on my rolling stool and dropped my head into my hands.

I had a massive fucking headache.

Preppy had organized this party for me, and the pre-prison me would've already been snorting blow off the tits of strippers. But post-prison me just wanted some food, a good night's sleep, and these fucking people to get the hell out of my house.

"You okay, boss-man?" Preppy asked, peeking his head into the room.

I pointed to the unconscious girl in the chair. "Come

get this bitch out of here." I ran my hand through my hair, the pulsing of the music making the pounding in my head grow stronger. "And for fucks sake, turn that shit down!" Preppy didn't deserve my rage, but I was too fucked up in the head to dial down my orders.

"You've got it," he said, without hesitation.

Preppy slid past me and didn't question the half-naked girl on the table. He hoisted her limp body over his shoulder in one easy movement. The unconscious girl's arms flailed around on his back, smacking against his back with each step. Before he could get too far, he turned back to me.

"You done with this?" he asked. I could barely hear him over the music. He gestured with his chin to the brunette on his shoulder, a childlike grin on his face.

I nodded, and Preppy smiled like I'd just told him he could have a puppy.

Sick fuck.

I loved that kid.

I closed the door, grabbing my gun and knife from the bottom drawer of the tool box I kept my tattoo equipment in. I sheathed my knife in my boot, and my gun in the waistband of my jeans.

I shook my head from side to side to clear away the haze. Prison will do that to you. Three fucking years sleeping with one eye open in a prison full of people with whom I've made both friends and enemies.

It was time to keep some of those friends and call in some of those favors, because there was something more important than my own selfish shit that I needed to take care of.

Someone more important.

Sleep could wait. It was time to go down stairs and make nice with the bikers. I'd avoided doing business with them in any capacity for years even though their VP, Bear, is like a brother to me. Bear tried to get me to join his MC a hundred times, but I'd always said no. I was a criminal who liked my crimes straight up, without a side of organized. But now I needed connections the bikers could provide as well as access to shady politicians whose decisions and opinions could be swayed for a price.

I never cared about money before. It used to be something disposable for me, something I used to fund my *I don't give a fuck* lifestyle. But now?

Payoffs to politicians didn't come cheap, and I was going to need a lot of cash and very fucking soon.

Or I was never going to see Max again.

Doe

Nikki was my one and only friend in the entire world.

And I kind of fucking hated her.

Nikki was a hooker who'd found me sleeping under a

bench. I'd unsuccessfully avoided the previous night's downpour and had just shivered and chattered myself to sleep. I'd already been living on the streets for several weeks at that point and hadn't had a real meal since running away from Camp Touchy-Feely, a nickname I gave the group home I'd been left to rot in. I'm pretty sure Nikki was trying to rob me—or what she thought was a corpse—when she just happened to have noticed I was still breathing.

Frankly, I'm surprised she even bothered with me after realizing I was very much alive.

Not so much living, but alive.

Nikki snorted the last of her blow through a rolled up post-it-note off a yellowed sink that was days away from falling free from the wall. The floor was littered with toilet paper, and all three toilets were on the verge of overflowing with brown sludge. The overwhelming scent of bleach singed my nose hairs like someone doused the room with chemicals to lessen the smell but hadn't bothered with any actual cleaning.

Nikki tilted her chin up toward the moldy ceiling tiles and pinched her nostrils together. A single fluorescent light flickered and buzzed above us, casting a greenish hue over the gas station bathroom.

"Fuck, that's good shit," she said, tossing the empty baggie onto the floor. Using the wand from an almost empty tube of lip-gloss, she fished out whatever was left and applied it to her thin cracked lips. She then smudged the thick liner under her eyes with her pinky until she nodded in satisfaction into the mirror at her racoon-esque smoky look.

I stretched my sleeve of my sweater down over the heel of my hand and wiped the filth off the mirror in front of me, exposing two things: a spider web crack in the corner and the reflection of a girl I didn't recognize.

Light blonde hair. Sunken cheeks. Bloodshot blue eyes. Dimple chin.

Nothing.

I knew the girl was me, but who the fuck was I?

Two months ago, a garbage man discovered me in an alley where I had been literally thrown out with the trash, found lying in my own blood amongst a heap of garbage bags beside a dumpster. When I woke in the hospital, with the biggest fucking headache in the history of headaches, the police and doctors dismissed me as a runaway. Or a hooker. Or some hybrid combo of the two. The policeman asking me questions at my bedside didn't bother to hide his disgust when he informed me that what probably happened was a simple case of a John getting rough with me. I'd opened my mouth to argue but stopped.

He could've been right.

Nothing else made any sort of sense.

No wallet. No ID. No money. No possessions of any kind.

No fucking memory.

When someone goes missing on the news, teams of people gather together and form a search party. Police reports are filed and and sometimes candlelight vigils are held in hopes the missing would soon return home. What they don't ever show you is what happens when no one looks. When the *loved ones* either don't know, don't exist...or just don't care.

The police searched the missing persons reports throughout the state and then the country with no luck. My fingerprints didn't match any on record, and neither did my picture.

I learned then that being labeled a missing person didn't necessarily mean I was missed. At least not enough to require any of the theatrics. No newspaper articles. No channel-six news. No plea from family members for my safe return.

Maybe, it was my fault no one had bothered to look for me. Maybe, I was an asshole and people celebrated the day I went away.

Or ran away.

Or was shipped down river in a fucking Moses basket.

I don't fucking know. Anything was possible.

I don't know where I came from.

I don't know how old I am.

I don't know my real name.

All I had in the world was reflected back at me in the bathroom mirror of that gas station, and I had no fucking clue who she was.

Without knowing if I was a minor or not, I was sent to live at Camp Touchy-Feely, where I only lasted a couple of weeks among the serial masturbators and juvenile delinquents. On the night I woke up to find one of the older boys standing at the foot of my bed with his fly unzipped, his dick in his hand, I escaped through a bathroom window. The only thing I left with was the donated clothes on my back, and a nickname.

They called me Doe.

As in Jane Doe.

The only difference between me and a real Jane Doe was a toe-tag because what I was doing sure as shit wasn't living. Stealing to eat. Sleeping wherever I could find cover from the elements. Begging on the side of freeway off-ramps. Scrounging through restaurant dumpsters.

Nikki ran her chewed-off fingernails through her greasy red hair. "You ready?" she asked. Sniffling, she hopped on the balls of her feet like she was an athlete amping up for the big game.

Though it was the furthest thing from the truth, I nodded. I wasn't ready, never would be, but I'd run out of options. It wasn't safe on the streets, each night in the open was a literal gamble with my life. And not to mention that if I lost any more weight, I wouldn't have the strength to fight off any threats. Either way I needed protection from both the elements and the people who lurked around at night before I ended up a real Jane Doe.

I don't think Nikki was capable of registering the feeling of hunger. Given the option, she chose a quick high over a full stomach. Every single time. A sad fact made obvious by her sharp cheekbones and dark circles under her eyes. In the short time I'd known her, I'd never seen her ingest anything but coke.

I judge her and I feel shitty about it. But something inside me tells me that she's better than the thing she does. When I'm not extremely irritated with her I feel almost protective of her. I was fighting for my own survival and I wanted to fight for hers, but the problem was, she didn't want to fight for herself.

I opened my mouth to lecture her. I was about to tell her that she should lay off the dope and change her main priority to food and her overall health, when she turned toward me. There I was, my mouth agape, ready to rain down judgment on her regarding like I was better than her. The truth was that I could've been knee deep involved in the same shit before I lost my memory.

I closed my judgmental mouth.

Nikki eyed me up and down, appraising my appearance. "I guess you'll do," she said, blatant dissatisfaction in her tone. I refused to cake on makeup or pluck out all of my eyebrows just to draw a thin line in their place like she did. Instead, I'd washed my hair in the sink and used the hand dryer to speed along the drying process. My face was makeup free, but it would have to do, because if I was going to do this, I was determined to do it my way and without looking like Nikki.

Yep, I am a judgmental asshole.

"How is this going to work again?" I asked. She'd already told me ten times, but she could tell me ten thousand times and I still wouldn't feel comfortable.

Nikki fluffed out her limp hair. "Seriously, Doe, do you ever listen?" She sighed in annoyance but continued on. "When we get to the party all you have to do is cuddle up to one of the bikers. If he likes you there is a good chance he might want to take you in, keep you around for a while, and all you have to do is keep his bed warm and a smile on his face."

"I don't know if I can do it." I said meekly.

"You can do it, and you will do it. And don't be all shy like that around them, they won't like that. Besides, you're not the shy type, that's just your nerves talking. You're all rough edges, especially with that horrible case of foot-in-mouth syndrome."

"It's eerie how you have me pegged in the short time you've known me," I said.

Nikki shrugged. "I'm a people reader, and believe it or not, you are very easy to read. Like for example, right now you're super tense. I know this because your shoulders are all hunched over." She presses my shoulders back. "Better. Stick out your chest. You don't have much to work with up top but without a bra, if you keep your shoulders back, they can catch a glimpse of a little nip, and guys love the nips."

That was it. I could get a biker to like me, he would protect me, hopefully long enough for me to figure out plan B. "Worst case scenario is that he's only looking for a quick one-time thing and he'll throw you a few bucks and send you on your way." Nikki made it sound more like a vacation than prostitution.

I could fool myself into thinking that if I wasn't soliciting on the street then I wasn't like Nikki, but the truth was no matter which way I twisted the facts, this plan would turn me into a whore.

Judgey McJudgerpants.

When I wracked my brain for other options, I'd come up as empty as my stomach.

Nikki pushed open the door, and sunlight invaded the dark space as it swung back and forth. With one last glance at the plain-faced girl in the mirror, I whispered, "I'm sorry."

It was a comfort knowing that whoever I was before my slate was wiped clean didn't know what I was about to do.

Because I was about to sell her body.

And whatever soul I still had.

CLICK HERE TO READ MORE OF KING

A MESSAGE FROM THE AUTHOR

In this book I mention a casino on an Indian reservation, but I do not mention the name of the tribe. This is intentional. I did not want to create an imaginary tribe in fear of offending existing ones, and I did not want to use the name of an existing one in fear of the same, as well as a fear of not being able to describe it well enough to do it justice. The tribe, reservation, and casino in this book are entirely of my own imagining. The rituals performed in this book are a product of combining research on the ceremonies and rituals from several different tribes, and for that reason, entirely fictional.

I also take a lot of artistic liberties when it comes to the town, my characters, medical interventions, and most other things. I do this because my goal is not to keep things realistic, it's to create an entire world existing within, yet entirely separate, from the real world.

And because it's fiction.

And because I do what I want.

Word to your mother,

-T.M.

ACKNOWLEDGMENTS

To be able to write stories for a living means everything to me. It is all because of YOU my wonderful readers who continue to buy and devour my books with an enthusiasm that makes me more and more emotional with each release. I can't thank you enough.

Thank you to Karla Nellenbach and Ellie for assistants with edits and proofing. Without you there would be no commas. Or too many commas. I hate commas. Whatevs.

Thank you to my agent, Kimberly Brower, for taking a chance on me all those years ago. Look how far we've come!

Thank you to all of my foreign publishers for bringing my words to your country and introducing my stories to the world.

Thank you to Wander Aguilar for your amazing talent. Your photos are inspirational, as are you, my friend.

Thank you to Jenn and Sarah of Social Butterfly PR for being the best PR team out there, as well as my friends.

Thank you to BB Easton, as always, for putting up with my whining and crying.

Thank you to my beta readers and my ARC team. You guys are the best. I couldn't do this without you. Sarah Sentz, you are an angel.

Thank you to my Frazierlanders for being my safe place and my favorite people.

A huge and very special thank you to the other half of my love story. Logan, I know it's not easy being married to a woman who literally hears people talking in her head. Thank you for taking care of us when I can't. Thank you for understanding when I have dark days out of nowhere. Thank you for knowing that lighter days always follow. Not a lot of people could deal with a spouse who works crazy hours and whose mind is usually somewhere else. Not only do you put up with me, but you love me for it, not in spite of it. Without your encouragement and support none of these books would have ever been written, and I would never have discovered who I truly am. For that alone I owe you the world. Thank you for not only pushing me to embark on this incredible journey, but for taking it with me. I love you forever and always, with everything I am and more. I couldn't write about love if you hadn't shown me what it really means.

Thank you to my baby girl for just being you. Mommy loves you to the moon and back.

ALSO BY T.M. FRAZIER

THE PERVERSION TRILOGY

PERVERSION (Book 1)

POSSESSION (Book 2)

PERMISSION (Book 3)

THE OUTSKIRTS DUET

THE OUTSKIRTS (Book 1)

THE OUTLIERS (Book 2)

THE KING SERIES

LISTED IN RECOMMENDED READING ORDER

Jake & Abby's Story (Standalone)

The Dark Light of Day (Prequel)

King & Doe's Story (Duet)

KING (Book 1)

TYRANT (Book 2)

Bear & Thia's Story (Duet)

LAWLESS (Book 3)

SOULLESS (Book 4)

Rage & Nolan's Story (Standalone)
ALL THE RAGE (Spinoff)

Preppy & Dre's Story (Triplet)
PREPPY PART ONE (Book 5)
PREPPY PART TWO (Book 6)
PREPPY PART THREE (Book 7)

Smoke & Frankie's Story (Standalone)
UP IN SMOKE (Spinoff)

COMING IN 2019

NINE, THE TALE OF KEVIN CLEARWATER

ABOUT THE AUTHOR

T.M. Frazier never imagined that a single person would ever read a word she wrote when she published her first book. Now, she's a USA Today bestselling author. Her books have been translated into numerous languages and published all around the world.

She's still in a state of shock.

T.M. enjoys writing what she calls 'wrong side of the tracks' romance with sexy, morally corrupt anti-heroes and ballsy heroines.

Her books have been described as raw, dark and gritty. Basically, what that means, is while some authors are great at describing a flower as it blooms, T.M. is better at describing it in the final stages of decay.

She loves meeting her readers, but if you see her at an event please don't pinch her because she's not ready to wake up from this amazing dream.

For more information please visit her website www.tmfrazierbooks.com

Come visit me in Frazierland, my reader group on Facebook! www.facebook.com/groups/tmfrazierland.

FACEBOOK: facebook.com/tmfrazierbooks
TWITTER: twitter.com/tm_frazier
INSTAGRAM: instagram.com/t.m.frazier

44264937R00130

Made in the USA
Columbia, SC
19 December 2018